THE BODY POLITIC

CATHERINE AIRD

The Body Politic

A CRIME CLUB BOOK
DOUBLEDAY
New York London Toronto Sydney Auckland

A Crime Club Book
PUBLISHED BY DOUBLEDAY
a division of Bantam Doubleday Dell Publishing Group, Inc.
666 Fifth Avenue, New York, New York 10103

DOUBLEDAY and the portrayal of a man
with a gun are trademarks of Doubleday,
a division of Bantam Doubleday Dell
Publishing Group, Inc.

Library of Congress Cataloging-in-Publication Data

Aird, Catherine, pseud.
The body politic/Catherine Aird.
    p. cm.
"A Crime Club book."
I. Title.
PR6051.I65B6   1991
832'.914—dc20   91-105
CIP

ISBN 0-385-41780-2
Printed in the United States of America
September 1991
First Edition in the United States of America

10 9 8 7 6 5 4 3 2 1

For Arnie *et al.*
donum memoriae causa

THE BODY POLITIC

The chapter headings are taken from *Dominus Illuminatio Mea* by R. D. Blackmore

ONE

In the Hour of Death

"WHY DON'T YOU drop dead?"

The question came from somewhere over on Peter Corbishley's right and he wasn't quite sure at first whether he had actually heard it at all or whether it had just been a figment of his imagination. The current Parliamentary session had, after all, been an unusually hard and tiring one.

This last doubt, at least, was resolved almost immediately.

"I said," repeated the voice with unmistakable clarity, "why don't you drop dead?"

This time there was no possibility that Peter Corbishley had been dreaming: he had heard the voice all right. And there was no confusion about whence the voice had come either: its owner was a man standing near the back of his audience and slightly to the right of the assembled company. Peter Corbishley picked him out of the crowd without difficulty as soon as he spoke for the second time. When he had pinpointed the man's position in the crowd, Corbishley felt a little happier. He was a great believer in the old aphorism "know thine enemy," and at least he knew now from where the man was standing that he was dealing with an experienced heckler.

The interrupter's location in this particular quarter of the group came as no great surprise to the Member of Parliament for the East Berebury division of the County of Calleshire. Practised hecklers were traditionally to be found on the fringes of a politician's audience. Even a Sunday morning orator from Speakers' Corner in

London's Hyde Park knew that. It was the inexperienced trouble-makers who made the elementary mistake of sitting in the front row where they were much more easily contained by stewards and, more importantly, placed where almost no one in the audience could hear them or see what they were up to.

Since on his part Peter Corbishley was an experienced speaker too, he did not even turn his head in the man's direction but, instead, carried on with his prepared oration. This did not mean, though, that he didn't go on thinking about the interrupter.

It wasn't that he was at all put out by the heckler—Peter Corbishley had been the sitting Member for the East Berebury constituency of Calleshire for nearly twenty years now and was therefore pretty well inured to interruption by both political friend and political foe, to say nothing of Mr. Speaker—only that he was faintly surprised by the actual occasion at which the man had chosen to voice his feelings. The annual summer garden party at Mellamby—for that was what it really was—had been traditionally always more of a social event than a political one.

"Why don't you drop dead?" The voice came again in just the same tone.

The meeting at the village of Mellamby had never been exactly a fireworks party. Political platitudes followed by strawberries and cream summed up the afternoon quite well as a rule.

Never raspberries, so to speak.

Until now, that is.

Peter Corbishley ignored both the heckler's remarks and his invitation to drop dead. Instead he tightened his grip on the notes in his hand and continued to deliver himself of his traditional end-of-the-summer session speech to the assembled members of the Mellamby and District Branch of the Berebury Conservative Association.

It was usually one of the quietest meetings in his constituency calendar, coming as it did when the school holidays were in sight and interest in affairs of state was yielding to anxieties about the harvest and the condition of the pound sterling on the foreign exchange. Medieval conflicts had seldom begun until the crops had been safely gathered in—Corbishley was something of an historian *manqué* and had made some studies of the causes of war and the timing of battles—and armchair economists, he had realised long ago, tended to take an instant stance on international fiscal policy only after they had bought their holiday travel currency.

What had led to the good turn-out of members at Mellamby this afternoon and therefore ensured the Member a worthwhile audience was not an interest in politics at all but the venue of the meeting. The annual summer meeting of the Branch of the Association was always held—by special invitation—at Mellamby Place, which was by far the grandest house in the neighbourhood. It was this, he knew perfectly well, rather than the presence of the Member of Parliament, which accounted for the floral dresses of the ladies and the tidy attire of their farmer husbands. It wasn't every day of the week by any means that the inhabitants of the village of Mellamby and its environs took afternoon tea on the terrace of Mellamby Place at the invitation of its owner.

Thus reminded, Peter Corbishley cast a covert glance at their host to see how he was taking the heckler's interruption.

Throughout the history of Calleshire the Raulys of Mellamby had been celebrated as men of action, and the present—and last—of that ilk, Bertram Millington Hervé Rauly, was no exception. Moreover, he belonged to that exalted class of persons who saw no need whatsoever to consult with anyone else at all before embarking on the course of action of his choice. And certainly not before holding a political meeting in his own grounds. The family motto, *Amicis quaelibert hora,* emblazoned above the splendidly embellished chimneypiece in the Great Hall of Mellamby Place meant that any hour was all right for friends. "And everyone else can go to hell," its owner was wont to add, when pointing it out.

So far, Peter Corbishley was happy to see, Bertram Rauly was sitting quietly on the little platform that had been improvised on the terrace on the south-facing aspect of the house. He was on the other side of the Branch Chairman, Major Derrick Puiver. Not, Peter Corbishley would have been the first to admit, that Bertram Rauly's apparent quietness meant that he wasn't contemplating action. Throughout history great landed proprietors have been notoriously sensitive to intruders of any nature, and Rauly might just be taking the man's measure or, rather less happily, measuring his distance.

The Chairman of the Branch Association was, the Member of Parliament knew, unlikely to be taking such a relaxed view. The

Major was a born worrier and, as such, admirably suited to have been in full command of a Supplies Depot in the Korean War. In his mind's eye Peter Corbishley could imagine the Major now running through a mental list of increasingly unfortunate scenarios. Like having a real nutter on their hands. Or worse. A zealot.

At least, thought the Member philosophically, it made a change from having barracking undergraduates from the University of Calleshire around. Cohorts of these were apt to turn up at his meetings; and not bent on the pursuit of pure learning either.

Actually, now he came to think about it, the heckler did look a little out of the ordinary. Assured the Bertram Rauly was at least sitting quietly for the time being—and only then—Peter Corbishley had allowed his gaze to drift in the direction of the man without its appearing to do so. The dissident member of the audience—he certainly wasn't a member of the Association if he behaved as he was doing—was thin and rather wild-looking and a little bit younger than Corbishley had expected. His hair was almost as long as a woman's and his voice shook with feeling as he shouted for the fourth time at Peter Corbishley.

"Why don't you drop dead?"

The Member of Parliament carried on with his speech with practised smoothness. The moment at which a public speaker acknowledged the existence of a heckler—if, indeed, he ever did—was a matter of fine political judgement, and the politician in Corbishley wanted to know what this particular heckler had in mind—beyond his, Peter Corbishley's, own immediate demise, that is—before he entered into any sort of dialogue with him.

"You heard me!" declared the heckler in tones designed to carry.

Since everyone present on the lawn in front of Mellamby Place, to say nothing of those attending to the preparation of the strawberry tea on neat little tables under the immemorial elm trees beyond, must also have heard what had been said, Peter Corbishley did not attempt to deny it. Instead he continued to expound his views on the Common Agricultural Policy of the European Community. The Member of Parliament automatically corrected his own train of thought as he did so.

It was only his views on the Common Agricultural Policy and its interventionist and set-aside practices which were fit to print that he was expounding. And by the well-known phrase "fit to print" he really meant that which he was prepared to see attributed to him in the local newspaper.

For a working politician Peter Corbishley was a fundamentally honest man.

A slight stirring to his left indicated to the Member that while Bertram Rauly might not be worried by sundry interruptions the Chairman of the Branch Association certainly was. Major Puiver liked everything cut and dried: it was this very characteristic that had made his operation in the field of supplies such a success. In those far-off days when the Major had gone to war there had been no such thing as a computer to help with the knotty classification of such essential items of modern warfare as "Bottles, water, rubber, hot, officers for the use of." Any capacity that the little Major might ever have had for dealing with the unexpected—a sudden run on winter battledress for instance—had withered and died long before he first drew his pension.

Peter Corbishley shot a quick glance at Major Puiver now and took in the fact that he had already started to perspire just a little along his hair line. The Member knew that it wasn't just the heat of a lovely summer's day that had caused the beads of sweat to appear. It was the lurking fear that a public pronouncement might become necessary which did that. The Major's gallantry was specific to the military and did not extend to public speaking. Like Demosthenes, he suffered from stage-fright.

The Member had been told more than once by David Chadwick, his Party Agent, that the Major's main anxiety as Chairman of the Mellamby Branch of the Association was that the official speaker would be late in arriving at a Branch meeting and he, Derrick Puiver, would have to extemporise on his carefully prepared Chairman's remarks to fill the gap.

Not that Peter Corbishley minded about this. What he really disliked were branch chairmen who *did* enjoy his delayed arrival and who then embarked on their own State of the Nation speech while the audience was waiting for the Member to arrive—and who didn't stop and sit down when he did. Corbishley had known the schedule of more whistle-stop tours of the constituency at election time to founder on this than on awkward questions from those in the audience.

The voice at the back became more strident. "I said, 'Why don't you drop dead?'"

The Member of Parliament might have deemed it prudent not to look in the heckler's direction. No such thought appeared to have occurred to Bertram Rauly. He was considering the man with the undisguised interest of a sportsman contemplating a new species of game. Of one thing Peter Corbishley was quite sure, and that was that nothing really worried Rauly, who had collected a DSO and an MC as a tank commander in the Western Desert for actions so flamboyant that it was rumoured that even Field-Marshal Rommel had been surprised. Peter Corbishley just hoped that the owner of Mellamby Place didn't happen to have a loaded gun too readily at hand.

The original owners of Mellamby Motte, the de Caquevilles, who were said to have come over with William the Conqueror, would never have been without a weapon of one sort or another within reach either. Corbishley spared a glance in the direction of the ruins of the great Norman keep beyond the house. Sited on a natural mound on the land, and given a licence to crenellate in 1272, the tower of the old castle still caught the eye. The occupants of Mellamby Motte would always have had oil on the boil, in a manner of speaking, against the arrival of unwelcome visitors.

And crossbows at the ready for enemies.

He brought his gaze back to the home of the Raulys. Mellamby Place was a fine Jacobean house set on a little plateau not far from the castle ruins. Its site, the historians said, was probably the jousting ground of the old castle: this view was lent further weight by the fact that the south lawn was still known as the tiltyard.

The only tournament that seemed to be engaged today was between one middle-aged and overworked Member of Parliament and an unknown heckler. Tomorrow, Peter Corbishley reminded himself, would be different. Tomorrow contemporary politics were to give way to the memory of an old battle. The Camulos Society were going to re-enact the celebrated clash between King Henry III and Simon de Montfort at the town of Lewes in Sussex in 1264.

Peter Corbishley would be there, of course, and would say a few words—had not Parliament itself come about because of Simon de

Montfort?—but it was today's proceedings that were his real concern just at this moment.

He corrected himself even as he turned over his written speech at an oblique and decidedly ambiguous reference to the Common Market's unfortunate "butter mountain." Mention of this and of the "wine lake" and similar economic embarrassments reminded him irresistibly of Hans Christian Andersen's Witch's Gingerbread House and other nursery stories of his childhood, and he skated quickly over the knotty problem of production surpluses in a sudden welter of words.

"Furthermore . . ." Even as the Member of Parliament spoke to an audience comprised mainly of farming families who had a keen interest in an agricultural policy of their own and who were therefore giving him their close attention, his own mind was elsewhere. The only part of today's proceedings which was really worrying him was a meeting he had lined up after tea with an anxious constituent.

"Why don't you drop dead?"

This time the Member scarcely heard the interruption to his speech. The person in the audience who was causing Peter Corbishley genuine concern was certainly not the heckler. Unless, that is, the heckler was called Alan John Ottershaw. Which he very much doubted.

Corbishley didn't even know Ottershaw by sight and so could not attempt to pick him out from among those sitting or standing in front of him. All that the Member of Parliament knew about Alan Ottershaw was that he was relatively young and—since he had just flown home from the Middle East, where he worked—probably the possessor of a good tan. He wasn't likely to recognise him anyway, since Ottershaw had always worked abroad and, as far as the Member knew, he had not met him before.

The man had married a girl from Mellamby and she had stayed on with their children in their house there: which was how it was that Alan Ottershaw came to be one of Peter Corbishley's constituents. At this particular moment the Member of Parliament could have wished Alan Ottershaw's English base had been anywhere else but the Parliamentary division of East Berebury in the County of Calleshire.

Or that he hadn't had the misfortune to have been involved in a road traffic accident in the Sheikhdom of Lasserta last week.

Peter Corbishley continued with the delivery of his speech, his mind dwelling on what he knew about Alan Ottershaw and his problems. A pedestrian had stepped out into the road in front of Alan Ottershaw's car in Lasserta, had been run over by the vehicle, and had died of his consequent injuries. An angry crowd of Lassertans, no lovers of expatriate mining engineers from the West at the best of times, had gathered round the luckless driver and made loud allegations of dangerous driving.

A charge of culpable manslaughter had been laid against Ottershaw with alarming speed. Well before any summons could be served, however, his employers, the giant Anglo-Lassertan Mineral Company, had spirited him swiftly out of the country and back to England. In Lasserta the penalty for killing either a man or a camel was death. (In certain highly specific circumstances the killing of a woman did not even rate as crime.)

So far, as the record went, so good.

Unfortunately the success of this manoeuvre had been very, very limited.

The real trouble had begun when the Lassertans had requested the immediate return of Alan Ottershaw to stand trial in Gatt-el-Abbas, the capital of Lasserta.

The Anglo-Lassertan Mineral Company's predictable stance on this had been that the presence of their employee was urgently required in their London office for consultations.

In that case, the Sheikh of Lasserta had decreed to Malcolm Forfar, the head of the firm in Wadeem, where the minehead was, the Anglo-Lassertan Mineral Company could remove itself from the Sheikhdom of Lasserta within forty-eight hours.

Before Malcolm Forfar could even draw breath the Sheikh had added a rider with a wolfish grin. "Or else . . ."

Forfar had waited, now quite unable to breathe.

"Or else," said the Sheikh, "its assets will be forfeit."

Reeling, the head of the firm had telexed London.

That had been on the Thursday afternoon, London time.

Ever since then the Board of the Anglo-Lassertan Mineral Company had been locked in deadly conclave in its prestige offices in

Mayfair. The fact that it was now forty-eight hours later and no balloon had yet gone up had been due solely to the good offices of Her Britannic Majesty's Ambassador in Lasserta.

Apprised of the situation by a distraught Malcolm Forfar, Mr. Anthony Mainwaring Heber Hibbs had demonstrated that he wasn't quite the old fuddy-duddy that the man from the mining company had always thought him. And that social and diplomatic skills, while not, naturally, in the same class of importance as mechanical expertise and experience, did have their place in the rich tapestry of international affairs.

Granted audience by the Sheikh of Lasserta without difficulty (happily he shared the Sheikh's interest in hawking), Mr. Heber Hibbs was far too wily a diplomat to attempt to discuss Alan Ottershaw and the road accident with Sheikh Ben Mirza Ibrahim Hajal Kisra. Instead, the Ambassador, who had learned a thing or two besides games on the playing fields of Eton, concentrated his efforts entirely on persuading the Sheikh to extend the time period of the ultimatum. Shotgun decisions did not as a rule leave room for manoeuvre, and room for manoeuvre was undoubtedly what the Anglo-Lassertan Mineral Company needed at this moment.

Anthony Heber Hibbs achieved this in a somewhat oblique way. While not going quite so far as actually to equate the traditional English "le weekend" with the Festival of Ramadan, the Ambassador did somehow manage to imply that Saturdays and Sundays were days in which it would be difficult to get reasoned responses out of a board of directors in London.

And the Sheikh, he skilfully inferred, was far too sensible a ruler to want a hasty or ill-considered response from men whom it might be difficult to call together if they were already dispersing to the country to prepare to read the lesson in their parish churches the next day. With real artistry he elevated the carving of roast beef at Sunday luncheon to an important ritual, while Yorkshire pudding and gravy found their way into his discourse as vague sorts of libation.

Sheikh Ben Mirza Ibrahim Hajal Kisra, who knew and liked Heber Hibbs, graciously allowed himself to be charmed into extending his deadline to seven days without loss of face. With the studied politeness customarily extended by members of his tribe to infidels he said, as he summoned his falconer with a flick of an imperious finger, "Is that not what you call a stay of execution?"

Her Britannic Majesty's Ambassador bowed.

TWO

After This Life's Whim

ALAN OTTERSHAW was a mining engineer who knew a great deal about the rare mineral known as queremitte but very little about the ways of international politics. He had, however, a touching faith, carefully nurtured among all employees, in the greatness and goodness of the company for which he worked. This faith lasted until exactly twenty minutes past four on the Friday afternoon after the road accident in Lasserta.

That was the moment when the Chairman of the Board, Hamer Morenci, asked the company's Director of Finance to give him a figure for the real value of the Anglo-Lassertan Mineral Company's assets in the Sheikhdom.

It was while the accountant was replying to this question that Alan Ottershaw had begun to feel uneasy. It had taken the money man a little while to explain that the company's holdings were practically incalculable except, naturally, for the purpose of writing down in the balance sheet and claiming depreciation allowances in the profit and loss account.

"Naturally," said Hamer Morenci, nodding.

As he listened to the Director of Finance it was gradually borne in upon Alan Ottershaw that, excellent servant of the company that he might be, he himself now figured on the debit side of the balance sheet. Like it or not, he had become a definite liability in the firm's eyes. And as the Director of Finance warmed to his theme and became even more eloquent on the subject of mine shafts and their role as written-down fixed assets in the company's accounts so Ottershaw's disquiet deepened.

"And then," put in Darren Greene, Vice-Chairman of the Board, in what Alan Ottershaw thought was an unnecessarily cold-blooded way, "there is the whole question of our monopoly rights in queremitte."

From the quality of the silence in the boardroom Ottershaw knew that nobody round the table had forgotten for one single moment that the Anglo-Lassertan Mineral Company leased the sole rights to mine under the Lassertan desert at Wadeem the only known seam of queremitte ore on the sunny side of the Iron Curtain.

The Chairman of the Board was not a diffident man—chairmen of international companies seldom are—but even he had the grace to look slightly embarrassed as he said, "I've got an appointment at the Ministry of Defence Procurement at six o'clock this afternoon." He coughed. "They have particularly requested that none of this reaches the press or, indeed, anyone else at all." He looked up. "No one knows that you're in the United Kingdom, do they, Ottershaw?"

"Nobody," said Alan Ottershaw evenly, shifting his stare from Darren Greene back to Hamer Morenci. "Not even my wife."

His initial disquiet was beginning to turn to real alarm now. A man didn't have to be a Kremlin-watcher to appreciate the significance of that remark of Morenci's about the Ministry of Defence Procurement. Normal businessmen would have been making their urgent appointments with the Foreign and Commonwealth Office. After-office-hours meetings at the Ministry of Defence Procurement late on a Friday afternoon in peacetime betokened very real alarm on both sides. The Anglo-Lassertan Mineral Company was certainly looking after its own interests with a vengeance. Alan Ottershaw, by then, had begun to feel it was high time someone looked after his.

"We have to consider the national interest, too, you see," added Morenci, whose own ethnic origins were a matter of perennial speculation both within and outside the firm.

That had been the point at which Ottershaw had felt truly frightened. As countless others before him had found to their cost, actions taken on those grounds could lead anywhere. Anywhere at all.

Which was how it came about that Peter Corbishley, the Member of Parliament for Alan Ottershaw's constituency, found himself studying his audience so carefully at the meeting at Mellamby the following afternoon. Sensing that the Board of the Anglo-Lassertan Mineral Company had reached the point of finding it difficult to discuss the realities of the situation with him underfoot, Alan Ottershaw had seized his moment and asked leave to depart to see his wife and children at his home in Calleshire.

Given his congé, the mining engineer had high-tailed it to Mellamby and made an urgent request to see his Member of Parliament as soon as possible. News could be embargoed from family and the press, but the sacred right of a citizen of the United Kingdom to communicate with his Member of Parliament was enshrined in custom and, in the case of mental hospitals and prisons, in the Rules and Regulations too.

With a rare serendipity it emerged that Peter Corbishley would actually be in Mellamby the very next afternoon and a meeting between the two men had been arranged for immediately after the strawberry tea. And, as far as Peter Corbishley was concerned, the sooner he was released from making speeches while someone unknown and quite probably unbalanced shouted at him to drop dead the better.

"Which brings me," the Member trilled fluently, "to the nub of my argument today—"

He was interrupted again but this time by a high mocking sound. It had the elements of laughter in it but no humour and it came from somewhere over by the trees.

"Ha, ha, ha, haaaaaaaaaaa, haa!"

Corbishley carried on valiantly. "As you will have appreciated, ladies and gentlemen—"

The eldritch noise came again. "Ha, ha, ha, haaaaaaaaaaaa, haa!"

Heads in the audience turned in the direction of the sound: some smiled, the more knowledgeable murmuring "woodpecker" to their neighbours before they turned back; but their concentration had gone.

"Why don't you drop dead?" asked his original tormentor, the heckler at the back of the audience; but he said it without conviction now.

The Member tried to finish on a rallying note, but the woodpecker would have none of it.

"Ha, ha, ha, haaaaaaaaaaa, haa!"

"Damned yaffle," said Bertram Rauly, trying to remember whether or not woodpeckers were a protected species these days.

Reminding himself that no actor could ever compete on stage with either children or animals, Peter Corbishley finished speaking and sat down amid polite applause. Major Puiver stood up, announced baldly that the Member had agreed to answer questions, and sat down again. There followed one of those uncomfortable pauses, common at all meetings of the party faithful everywhere, when no one spoke. Eventually a rather good-looking young man sitting near the front of the audience got to his feet and, with a distinct air of being a good man coming to the aid of the party, asked about precautions against rabies in the proposed Channel Tunnel.

Bertram Rauly leaned across Puiver and hissed in Corbishley's ear, "Adrian Dungey, local vet. Cocky."

The Member got to his feet and made an answer. Since if the young man was a veterinary surgeon he must have known what the Member's response was going to be, he kept it short, resumed his seat, and, there being no more questions from the audience, composed himself to listen to the vote of thanks. The gallant Major called upon Miss Mildred Finch to propose it and Bertram Rauly's expression became even more impenetrable.

As the Chairman sat down the Member stole an unobtrusive glance at his watch. Later on this evening he and Ted Sheard, the Labour Member of Parliament for West Berebury, were due at a Grand Charity Ball over at Calle Castle to launch a joint appeal for a hospice in the town of Berebury, and it would never do to be late for that.

Miss Finch, educated and articulate, thanked the Member for his clear exposition of his views on the Common Market without apparent irony and passed swiftly on to the Association's appreciation of their invitation that afternoon to one of the most beautiful houses in Calleshire. Mellamby Place was part of the inheritance of them all and of great importance in the history of the county—nay, of England itself. Had not King John himself hunted deer in Mellamby Chase where there were still trees so old as not to have been planted by the hand of man?

Its grounds, continued Miss Finch, hitting her stride now, were the home not only of *Picus viridis* but of many other creatures of the wild. (Puzzled faces cleared when it dawned on those of her audience who were actually listening that she meant the green woodpecker: the more sophisticated pretended that they had known all along.) As for the house, Miss Finch carried on, only slightly diverted by the sight of an ambulance with a flashing blue light disappearing towards the back entrance of Mellamby Place, it was a jewel in the County's crown and she hoped it would remain so whatever happened for ever . . .

"And a day," she finished triumphantly, leading the applause.

Thankfully the platform party dispersed.

The Chairman, Major Puiver, went in pursuit of the unknown heckler, with whom he wanted to have a few words, and who was even now shambling away at quite a rate and making it quite clear that he didn't want to speak to the Major: Bertram Rauly equally clearly wished to avoid having converse with Miss Mildred Finch and retreated back into Mellamby Place with almost indecent haste, pausing only to pick up something from the lawn. Whatever it was must have given him cause for thought, for he halted for a long moment, looking puzzled, then, keeping it—whatever it was—in his hand, he went indoors; while Peter Corbishley strolled across towards the tea table and his meeting with Alan Ottershaw.

He didn't have long to wait.

Minutes after Corbishley had prudently established himself near the tea urn a wiry young man was shaking him by the hand and introducing himself as Alan Ottershaw of Lasserta and Mellamby.

He put his problem to the Member a good deal more succinctly than most of Peter Corbishley's constituents.

"Can you," he said directly, "stop them sending me back to certain death?"

WHILE THE SATURDAY AFTERNOON had been sunny and warm, it was as nothing compared with the weather on the Sunday.

The day was one of those rare summer ones when the English climate was all that anyone could desire. This contributed in no small way to the success of the occasion of the Camulos Society's Summer Event, the re-enactment of the Battle of Lewes. The Honorary Secretary was up and about early enough to note the faint mist first thing in the morning and know it to be a portent of greater heat to come. He did spare a thought for those likely to spend the day in full—if imitation—armour and dismissed it almost at once. Fighting men expected to have to put up with a little discomfort in battle— even in mock battle.

The Secretary's main concern, and this was why he and his assistants were up and about betimes, was the marking out of the course, so to speak. Before the combatants arrived they needed to know who had held which ground before the Battle of Lewes had begun. It could, after all, hardly be called the drawing up of lines of battle after the event. Everything had to be clearly marked before the battleground was officially handed over to the Battle Commander and Starter, Major Puiver.

There was, too, a particular need for the Secretary to be careful on this occasion because of what had happened last time: no one could have called the Spring Meeting of the Camulos Society an unqualified success. It had been a re-enactment of the Battle of Waterloo in 1815 and it had gone sadly awry.

Today, resolved the Secretary hopefully, would be better. While Mellamby Motte was many miles away from Lewes in Sussex and in 1264 had been untouched by the tide of war, its remains and surrounding grounds bore sufficient resemblance to Lewes and the terrain there to make it a good spot for a replay.

Mellamby Motte had the added advantage that it was well out in the country and had plenty of open ground which could be used for the re-enactment of the battle.

It wasn't like that at Lewes any more.

The other great attraction of Mellamby was the enthusiastic co-operation of its owner. Bertram Rauly was a most active member of the Camulos Society and had himself drawn the Committee's attention to the similarity of the ground north of the old Motte to that at Lewes. Besides, not every landowner relished horses and men trampling over his ground, especially when they were attended by crowds of people, which as a rule did even more damage and certainly left more debris behind than any war. Casualties in a mock battle usually removed themselves tidily from the field: spectators always left litter.

"You'd better come while the going's good," Rauly had said at the

Society's committee meeting when the venues of next year's activities were being discussed. "God knows what'll happen to Mellamby when I'm gone."

Since Bertram Millington Hervé Rauly was unmarried and had no brothers, this remark had been greeted with tactful silence by most of the Committee and by the rapid production of his diary by the Chairman. "When can we come?" he asked.

A date had been duly fixed and had now arrived.

With the verisimilitude for which the Camulos Society was renowned, the Honorary Secretary sent his Assistant Secretary up to the top of Mellamby Motte with a Royal Standard of the day, and set off himself for some high ground to the north of the old castle, just short of Mellamby Chase, that was to serve as Offham Hill. Warning his confrère to take care inside the shaky old tower, he picked up the four markers which were to constitute the starting post before the "off" of the opposing side.

He frowned to himself as he made his way over the grass. Even as a schoolboy he had hesitated to think of Simon de Montfort as an enemy. He wouldn't have liked to have had to deal with King Henry III himself. It was easier with the re-enactment of the Wars of the Roses—you could choose to be a Yorkist or a Lancastrian without ceasing to be loyal to the English throne. And you could go over the Civil Wars again and again without losing sympathy with King Charles I (admittedly a poor monarch but a good family man) or being drawn to Oliver Cromwell (unattractive on almost every count, including the warts).

It was only the fact that some members of the Society also liked to be on the winning side that enabled the Camulos Society to rustle up enough Roundheads to stage some of the Civil War battles at all. Everyone wanted to be a Loyalist and nobody a Parliamentarian.

The Secretary struck a marker into the ground on the top of the rise. It was meant to indicate the point where Simon de Montfort had taken up his stance at the beginning of that day in May 1264. Although Montfort might well be said to have been the first Parliamentarian himself, there had been no shortage of members willing to play him. Montfort had had a better press than poor Nol Cromwell. Perhaps the warts had had something to do with that, too.

History might be bunk, thought the Secretary, but it was very curious all the same.

He turned and counted his paces as he stepped eastwards and a little south. Simon de Montfort's son, Henry, had drawn up with his men slightly ahead of his father and his force of men. De Montfort *père*, with a commendable restraint, had kept his own troops in reserve for the time and place where they were needed most.

The Secretary plunged the marker into the ground and continued his way eastwards. Gilbert de Clare, Earl of Oxford, had been on Henry de Montfort's left at the Battle of Lewes, but he'd changed sides after it and before the Battle of Evesham.

The Secretary tapped Gilbert de Clare's marker into the Calleshire soil with extra vigour. Turncoats were never popular roles in the Society, but someone had been found to take his part. The last marker was intended to represent the spot where Nicholas de Segrave had marshalled his force. There had been no touch of the renegade about Nicholas de Segrave and no trouble about finding a keen young Society member to don his colours.

Oddly enough, it had been the Royalist side that had been more difficult to cast in this battle: perhaps it was because they had been the losers.

What had also been as tricky as always had been finding suitable roles for the more mature members of the Society to play.

Especially Bertram Millington Hervé Rauly.

Common politeness to their host had prompted the suggestion on somebody's part that he should be King Henry III.

"After all," the youngest member of the Committee had added tactlessly, "the King was all of fifty-six at the time."

The Chairman of the Society, who would never see sixty-five again, had pointed out rather coldly that the King had fought valiantly and energetically all day even though he had finished it defeated and a prisoner.

"If Hazel Ottershaw is being Queen Eleanor, then Bertram's too old to be King anyway," said someone else flatly.

It had been the Honorary Secretary himself who had had the last word on who took the role of King Henry III. "Adrian Dungey has to be king," he said, "because he's the only one who can get into the royal armour."

Warwick the Kingmaker couldn't have done better.

"What about Bertram being Richard, Earl of Cornwall instead?" persisted the youngest member of the Committee.

"He ran away," said the Chairman.

"As well as being a first-class twit," said someone else.

"Prince Edward, then?" suggested the youngest Committee member, even though he had been hoping for the part himself. The dashing young man on the flying steed was a dream of a part to play.

"Forty years ago, yes," decreed the Chairman. "Now, no."

In the end they settled that Bertram Rauly should play the Royalist William de Wilton and thus be killed before luncheon.

THREE

When the Heart Beats Low

IT WAS THE BEST PART of ten days later before Detective Inspector C. D. Sloan heard anything about the Battle of Lewes, Mark II, and then only very obliquely.

Detective Inspector Sloan—for obvious reasons known as "Seedy" to his family and friends—was the Head of the Criminal Investigation Department of "F" Division of the Calleshire County Constabulary, and his headquarters were at the Police Station in the market town of Berebury. He lived in the town, too, and by virtue of this, as well as of his avocation, knew a good many of the other people who worked and had their being there.

He knew young Morton—always known as Tod—on both counts.

"Morning, Inspector." Young Morton might not have had his business clothes on, but he was still dressed with conspicuous formality for someone of his age.

"Morning, Tod."

"Got a minute?"

"For you, Tod, yes." Sloan had known Tod's father for years, and Tod himself ever since he was a lad. Morton and Sons were the oldest-established and best-run firm of funeral furnishers in Berebury, and one way and another Detective Inspector Sloan had had quite a lot to do with them in his time. Young Tod—although he wasn't as young as all that—was in the process of taking over the bulk of the work of the firm from his father in the best way possible for a son to step into his father's shoes. Unobtrusively.

Morton senior was still very much in evidence at all important funerals. Wearing his frock-coat complete with its velvet collar and carrying a black top hat and gloves, he continued to lead the way out of the church for the last journeys of the more distinguished citizens of the town. Nobody could deny that he had a certain gravitas which went well with ceremonial. Young Tod hadn't quite acquired that yet, although he was trying hard.

"Sit down." Sloan pointed to a chair. "How's trade?"

"Mustn't grumble."

"No . . ." Sloan knew farmers who had stopped grumbling about the weather because everyone expected them to complain, but he wasn't sure what worried undertakers. Miracle surgery, perhaps. He did know, though, that young Tod had just bought a new car that wasn't Berlin black in colour, so business couldn't be too bad.

"As long as folk don't take to sky burial," said Tod, "I reckon Morton and Sons'll be all right for a bit."

"Sky burial?" queried Sloan.

"The Chinese go in for it," said Tod.

"Bit of a contradiction in terms, isn't it?" hazarded Sloan curiously. "Sky burial."

"We're not really worried." Tod Morton grinned. "I don't think it'll ever really catch on in Calleshire. Besides, you need vultures."

"I get you. One dies, one lives." Even while he was speaking, Detective Inspector Sloan was casting his mind back over last week's sudden deaths in his patch. He couldn't remember any coming to police notice that might have caused Morton and Sons any difficulty. There hadn't even been a sticky inquest. "What can I do for you, Tod?" he asked with genuine interest.

"It's probably not important."

"All the better in my job," said Sloan, "if it isn't important."

He was a policeman, not a doctor. He actively preferred to be consulted about the trivial rather than the really significant. In his work the important usually meant that there was serious mischief to or by someone in the offing. He paused. Now that he came to think of it, so it did in the doctor's surgery too. He put the thought to the back of his mind for further consideration at some mythical period in the future when he had more time for philosophising and looked encouragingly in Tod Morton's direction.

"And it may be nothing," said that young sprig of the firm.

"You wouldn't have come to see me about nothing, Tod," said Sloan with inexorable logic.

Tod twisted his lips. "It's such a small thing . . ."

"Great oaks from little acorns grow," responded Sloan prosaically. Watergate had started with the tiniest leak: fingerprints weren't exactly large items either, and they had hanged many a murderer.

"So small," said Tod, "that it nearly got missed."

"Ah," said Sloan. So Tod had meant "small" literally.

The mortician put a hand in his pocket and brought out a matchbox which he laid with care on Sloan's desk without opening. "It's like this, Inspector."

"I'm all ears," said Sloan.

"By the time someone gets to be cremated——"

"A customer?"

"We prefer to call them 'clients.' "

"Client, then," said Sloan peaceably.

"These days," said the undertaker, "by the time he gets to be cremated, a client tends to have accumulated a fair bit of metal under his skin."

"Foreign bodies?"

"We do those, too, Inspector." Tod Morton very nearly pulled out a business card. "Had an Italian chap only the other day—his family wanted the full treatment."

"Not that sort of foreign body, Tod."

"They really understand about funerals in Italy," Tod said on a wistful note.

"They have a lot of them in the family," said Sloan drily. "Now, what is it that you want to show me?"

Tod leaned forward. "Like I was saying, Inspector, by the time a client gets to us, the hospital has often stuck a fair bit of metal into him one way and another."

Sloan nodded. It was a wonder that it wasn't known as "medical hardware."

"To say nothing of Kaiser Bill and old Adolf."

"What have they got to do with it?"

"Shrapnel," said Morton. "There's still a lot of it about from one war or another."

"Go on."

"Well, the relatives don't want what hasn't melted given back to them with the ashes, do they? Not unless it's precious metal and they don't get that back anyway."

"I suppose not." It was an aspect of cremation which hadn't occurred to Detective Inspector Sloan.

"Not very nice, some of the things the hospitals leave inside you." Tod Morton waved a hand. "Hips, knees——"

"Useful enough in life, though," pointed out Sloan.

"Very," agreed Tod swiftly. "Clever chaps, some of them up at the hospital. Not all of them, though," he added thoughtfully.

"These foreign bodies . . ."

"The cremation people have to remove them before the ashes go back to the relatives. Right?"

"I can see that they would have to."

"Believe you me," said Tod, "a hip joint is as big as a window catch."

"I believe you, Tod," said Sloan patiently.

"Looks a bit like one, too, come to that."

The sight of a replacement hip joint was something Sloan had been spared so far. But then he hadn't reached the age of spare-part surgery yet.

"And there's only the one way of collecting metal easily that I know," said Tod.

"A magnet."

"That's right, Inspector."

"So?"

"So even when the magnet gets to work on this client's ashes——"

"Which client, Tod?" prompted Sloan gently.

"Oh, didn't I say? Sorry. A man, name of Ottershaw. Alan John Ottershaw from Mellamby."

Sloan wrote that down. "Well?"

"This comes up." Tod Morton pointed to the matchbox but still made no move to open it.

"So?"

"It was in with the ashes when they gave me the urn at the crematorium." He flushed. "I sort of spilled them by mistake on my desk."

"And when they say they're Alan John Ottershaw's ashes, Tod, they mean it?"

" 'Course they do," said the young undertaker earnestly. "The cremator only does one at a time anyway so they couldn't be anyone else's. You can go and watch if you're an executor and feel strongly about that sort of thing. Have to, if you belong to some religions."

"All right then. So you collect the ashes of the late A. J. Ottershaw and what comes up?"

Tod shook his head. "Ah, there you have me, Inspector. I don't know what it is."

"All you know is that it isn't made of ferrous metal."

"Do I? Oh, yes, I've just said that the magnet goes over the ashes first, haven't I?"

"You have."

"Then it isn't easily crushable either," said Tod, "because the remains are reduced by crushing after that."

"What isn't?" prompted Sloan.

Tod became diffident again. "It may be nothing at all, of course."

"It can't be nothing," said Sloan logically.

"Well, an Oriental dental filling or something fancy like that. They said he'd been working abroad."

"But it may not be," reasoned Sloan. "You wouldn't have brought it here to show me unless there was a chance that it wasn't nothing, would you?"

A pedant might have had some trouble with that convoluted statement, but young Tod Morton knew exactly what Sloan meant. "No," he agreed at once. "That's true. I wouldn't."

"So?"

The matchbox still lay on Sloan's desk between the two men. Tod Morton, though, made no move to open it, but instead continued with his narrative. "So I showed it to Dad."

"And what did he say?" Tod's father was the grandson of the eldest son in the firm of Morton and Sons and knew the undertaking business backwards.

"That you can't be too careful these days."

Sloan nodded. It was a philosophy that had held good through the ages and doubtless helped account for the business longevity of Morton and Sons as well as many a more famous House.

"What with umbrella guns and that sort of thing," added Tod.

Progress took strange forms: Detective Inspector Sloan would be one of the first to admit that. "And what," he enquired, "did you do after that?"

"Tried to find out what the guy—the client, that is—was supposed to have died from."

"Ah." Sloan jerked his head. "And that's sometimes easier said than done, I suppose."

"It wasn't difficult, Inspector." Tod looked surprised. "The funeral director collects the medical forms from the doctors so he sees the cause of death then, but I had a word with Fred Tompkins anyway."

"Who's Fred Tompkins?"

"The mortuary porter at the hospital."

"Good idea," said Sloan warmly. Administrators and doctors never told anybody anything in case it was used in evidence afterwards. In Sloan's experience, not only did ward-maids and hospital porters usually, but not always of course, have the beans—well, some of them, anyway—but, more importantly, were nearly always prepared to spill them if they had.

Especially to an old friend.

"Fred said," carried on Tod Morton, "that this guy had snuffed it from a heart attack. Not anything out of the ordinary."

"Or we'd have heard," responded Sloan with confidence. "And there haven't been any coroners' inquests in Berebury for a couple of weeks now."

"Not even medically unusual, Inspector," said Tod, waving a hand to encompass the whole Police Station. "Let alone your sort of unusual."

"Ah." The medically unusual was only interesting to the Criminal Investigation Department if it arose from illegal homicide in any shape or form. Or criminal negligence. Nature could do her worst and leave the police unaffected. And often did.

It was funny how people never thought of her as Mother Nature then; that was when they remembered the "red in tooth and claw" bit.

"The only thing that was at all out of the way was that this guy Ottershaw had just come back from abroad."

"Had he?" That might well put a different complexion on what was in the matchbox. "Whereabouts abroad?"

"The Middle East," Tod Morton said. "He worked in the Sheikhdom of Lasserta."

"I see." Sloan drew a doodle on his notebook.

"Mining engineer, he was."

"It would say so on the cremation form, I suppose," said Sloan.

"Not only that," said Tod expansively, "but Fred said that the wife had told the doctors that he worked with some odd metal out there."

"Lasserta." Sloan cast about in his mind for whatever else came from the Middle East as well as crude oil. He had heard that they mined something else unusual in that part of the world and nowhere else, but he couldn't now remember what it was.

"Fred Tompkins didn't know what this stuff was called but he did know that the doctors had talked to the Health and Safety people in case there was something tricky about this particular ore that they ought to have known about."

"And was there?"

"Not that they knew," said Tod, twitching his shoulders expressively. "Which doesn't mean much, does it? Dad says some of them don't even know which way is up."

"Didn't they have a post-mortem?"

Tod shook his head. "Seems there was a doctor at this "do" out at Mellamby that Ottershaw collapsed at. He told the ambulance people that it was a heart attack and to get a move on."

"But it was no go?"

"That's right," said Tod. "He was unconscious but alive when they got to the hospital but he didn't last long. Fred said they had him in their Coronary Care Unit but it didn't do him any good."

Sloan leaned back in his chair. "So what brings you, Tod?"

Morton pointed to the matchbox. "That, Inspector. Whatever it is."

"Surprise me," invited Detective Inspector Sloan.

Morton opened the matchbox with all the concentration of a schoolboy with a captured Camberwell Beauty butterfly, teased a little wad of cotton-wool to one side and said, "There, Inspector. Look."

Sloan looked. What he saw was a very small metal pellet.

"The trouble," said Tod Morton, "is that——"

"It's hollow," finished Detective Inspector Sloan for him.

FOUR

And the Eyes Grow Dim

"LOOKING FOR WORK, are you, Sloan?" barked Police Superintendent Leeyes.

"No, sir."

"Because if you haven't got enough to do, you can get on with a bit of collar-fingering down in that new shopping arcade in the High Street."

"It's not that at all, sir."

"They tell me that there's a young woman down there doing that new thing which someone was trying to explain to me."

"Sugging, sir."

"Sounds foreign to me."

"It isn't, sir." The Superintendent's xenophobia was a by-word in the Calleshire Force. "It goes on all the time."

Leeyes sniffed. "I've never heard of it, Sloan, but then I've only been in the thief-taking business all my life."

"It stands for 'selling under guise,' sir."

"That poet fellow—you know who I mean, Sloan."

"Kipling, sir?" The Superintendent was a great one for attending Adult Education Classes in the long winter evenings. The sessions on "Rudyard Kipling—The Man and the Writer," had made a great impression on him.

"That's the fellow. You remember what he said, Sloan, don't you?"

" 'The crimes of Clapham are chaste in Martapan,' " said Sloan.

The entire complement of the Berebury Police Station knew the quotation by heart now. Actually Detective Inspector Sloan, rosarian when off-duty, had even looked it up once and found the line before that one even more interesting: "The wildest dreams of Kew are commonplace in Katmandu." He'd like that.

"Sugging," said Superintendent Leeyes firmly, "sounds more like Martapan than Clapham to me."

"It isn't, sir," insisted Sloan. "It's going about with a clipboard and a questionnaire pretending you're doing a survey and then, when you've got the person's name and address, trying to sell them something."

Leeyes scowled. "Having craftily found out first whether they can afford it."

"And if they're the sort of person likely to be in the market for that particular item," said Sloan. "Yes."

"Clever stuff," pronounced Leeyes. It was the ultimate accolade.

"I'll see to this woman," Sloan promised. "Now, sir, about this hollow pellet that Tod Morton—er—retrieved from some ashes." He explained what had been discovered in the cremated remains of Alan Ottershaw of Mellamby.

"Ottershaw, did you say?" grunted Leeyes. "Never heard of him. Anything known?"

"Not in the police sense," said Sloan cautiously, adding, "yet."

"And what, pray, is that supposed to mean?" enquired the Superintendent at his most Churchillian.

"I did a bit of asking about over at Mellamby where he came from, sir."

Leeyes frowned. "Who is our man there at the moment?"

"Constable Turton. He covers all the villages out that way."

"He's young, isn't he?"

"Yes, sir." The Superintendent had reached an age when youth had become an indictment in itself.

"Go on, Sloan. Tell me he's keen as well."

"He told me, sir," said Detective Inspector Sloan with quite a different emphasis, "that Alan Ottershaw had come home unexpectedly from the Middle East because of some trouble out there."

"There's always some trouble out there," declared Leeyes profoundly. "You've only got to look at yesterday's newspaper or in the Old Testament. Take your pick."

"Yesterday's newspaper?" said Sloan, wondering if he'd missed something he should have seen. "Was there a——"

"It's always the same," said Leeyes loftily. " 'Trouble in the Middle East'."

"Quite so," said Sloan, deciding that the Superintendent was taking the broad historical view: Leviticus to Mossadeq—if not later—so to speak. "Actually, this chap Ottershaw had just come back from Lasserta."

"Lasserta?" Superintendent Leeyes cocked his head alertly. "That's where we get our queremitte from, isn't it?"

Sloan gave an inward sigh. The Superintendent's knowledge was as quixotic as his ignorance. Both were quite unpredictable. There was no more reason why he shouldn't have known about sugging than that he did know about the ore from which queremitte was extracted.

"Can't do without queremitte," pronounced Leeyes briskly. "The Defence people need it for one of their fancy new weapons, don't they? Stands very high temperatures or something when it's put with something else."

"Yes, sir." Sloan nodded. "I don't know the fine detail but I'm told that it's a synergic agent absolutely essential for one whole range of weaponry." He gave a wry smile. "And I can confirm that it stands very high temperatures."

Leeyes grunted. "And has this got anything to do with the—er—deceased?"

"I don't know, sir. All I know is that a very small hollow pellet was included in the urn containing his cremated remains, which were to be delivered to his widow for interment."

"Not a lot to go on, Sloan, is it?"

"No, sir." He coughed. "And when the undertaker enquired what the cause of death had been——"

"The official cause of death," interjected Superintendent Leeyes cynically. His view of the medical profession was decidedly less than reverential.

"The official cause of death," amended Sloan, "the undertaker was told that it was thought to have been due to heart failure and certified accordingly."

Leeyes grunted.

Sloan hurried on. "The only complaint by anyone so far, sir, seems to have been about the length of time the ambulance took to get out of Mellamby."

"Busy with Inspector Harpe's Sunday afternoon smash-ups, were they?" suggested Leeyes pleasantly. Inspector Harpe was in charge of Traffic Division at Berebury, and that meant that road accidents were his pigeon.

"The ambulance people had had a rush turn-out the day before to the same place," said Sloan. "In response to some cock-and-bull story about the Member of Parliament having had a heart attack after a load of hassle with a heckler."

Leeyes made an enigmatic sound that could have meant anything.

"They chalked it up as a false alarm, malicious intent," said Sloan, "but, human nature being what it is, I daresay they didn't hurry the second time." They knew quite a lot at the police station about human nature being what it was.

"For the real thing?"

"According to Tod Morton, sir, yes." Sloan saw no reason to mention Fred Tompkins, the hospital porter. "I haven't seen the death certificate myself yet."

"But all of this was before this—er—alleged pellet was found?" Nobody had ever been able to say that Superintendent Leeyes hadn't got a clear eye for essentials.

"Yes, sir."

"Ahah."

"The doctors don't know about the pellet yet, sir." Sloan cleared his throat and explained conscientiously, "Of course, a heart attack may well have killed him as they say it did. We don't know."

"Are you trying to tell me, Sloan," grated Leeyes, "and not very clearly, if I may say so, that there was no post-mortem examination of the deceased?"

"I am, sir."

Leeyes grimaced. "So when you said you hadn't got a lot to go on, Sloan, you meant it literally?"

"I did."

"H'm," said Leeyes. His professional relationship with Dr. Dabbe, the consultant pathologist to the Berebury and District Hospital Management Group, was a stormy one to say the least, but the Superintendent always took due note of the doctor's post-mortem findings with the grudging respect of one specialist to another.

"Just this pellet, sir, that's all. And," he reminded his superior officer, "there may well be a perfectly innocent explanation for its having been in Ottershaw's body in the first place."

"I daresay," growled Leeyes, "that any defence counsel you care to mention could come up with six before breakfast, but that hasn't got anything to do with it, Sloan, has it?"

"No, sir." Detective Inspector Sloan assented to this promptly. What the Superintendent had said was perfectly true: if there was even one possible explanation that was not an innocent one, then the police had a duty to explore it. "I'm afraid that this pellet is all there is at the moment."

"What about the cremated remains?" As always the Superintendent's view was a literal one. "You've got them, haven't you?"

"Mortons, the undertakers, have them," replied Detective Inspector Sloan carefully. "I'm not quite sure what our legal standing is with regard to the ashes at this precise juncture."

"Stop talking like a solicitor, Sloan, and get on with it."

"But I do know that the undertakers haven't actually despatched them to the family yet. Young Tod Morton promised to hang on to them for a bit."

"That's something, I suppose," allowed Leeyes.

"But they will have to hand them over to the family fairly shortly, sir, unless . . ." He let the rest of the sentence trail away unfinished.

"What is their ultimate destination?" demanded the Superintendent. "Does young Morton know that?" He scowled. "Is the widow going to keep them on the mantelpiece in her egg-timer or anything silly like that?"

"I understand, sir," rejoined Sloan, "that there is a small area of churchyard outside the east window of St. Martin's Church at Mellamby reserved solely for the interment of ashes."

"Hrrrrrrmph."

Sloan hurried on. "Tod Morton tells me that Mrs. Ottershaw had asked him to arrange for her husband's ashes to be placed there in—er—due course."

"Mine," said the Superintendent unexpectedly, "are going to be scattered over the Berebury Golf Course."

"Really, sir?" Sloan managed to keep his face straight with difficulty.

"The eighteenth fairway," said Leeyes.

And Sloan managed to refrain from saying that it was more the date of the ceremony than the last resting place of his ashes that would interest the Superintendent's underlings at Berebury Police Station.

"Just where a good second wood shot from the tee reaches," amplified Leeyes, "with a following wind, of course."

"Naturally," concurred Sloan. Presumably a good following wind came in handy when ashes were scattered, too.

"It's a very tricky approach to the green from there, Sloan."

"Talking of tricky approaches, sir——" Sloan tried to seize his moment.

"And I never seem to quite get the distance."

"—I think we ought to be on the safe side, sir, and——"

"It's too far for a number seven iron."

"—talk to the Coroner," persisted Sloan. "Just in case."

"And too near for a number five."

"What about a number six?" suggested Sloan involuntarily—and immediately regretted doing so. When Queen Victoria had complained about the number of sparrows in the Crystal Palace, the Duke of Wellington had said, "Try sparrowhawks, ma'am," but then he had won the Battle of Waterloo and he was Prime Minister at the time. Police Superintendent Leeyes might not feel the same way about being advised by one of his detective inspectors.

Especially by someone who did not even play golf.

Which, as Sloan understood it, meant that he was not so much off the green as beyond the orange pale.

"Never carry a number six iron," retorted Leeyes speedily. "Of course you must talk to the Coroner, Sloan."

"Yes, sir."

"After you've found out how long this pellet had been in the body."

"Naturally, sir."

"If you can."

"Of course, sir."

"If it was while the deceased had been playing Cops and Robbers at the age of twelve or had a friend learning to use an air rifle at fourteen, then I don't think we need be too interested."

"No, sir."

"But if it was the week before he died, we are."

"Yes, sir."

"You'll have to talk to the metal specialists first."

"Yes, sir. I've already asked Sergeant Gelven to find out when queremitte was first mined and so forth."

"Gelven?" Superintendent Leeyes jerked his head up. "You can't have Sergeant Gelven. They're short on the detective side this week over at Calleford and they need a good man. He's reporting there first thing in the morning."

"I see, sir. Sorry, sir, I didn't know."

"You'll have to make do with Crosby."

"Yes, sir." Detective Inspector Sloan sighed. "I'm afraid the investigation may take a little longer then. I don't think Crosby has had any experience with either ballistics or heavy metals."

Detective Constable W. E. Crosby was the newest member of the Criminal Investigation Department at Berebury Police Station—and the most jejune.

"Then it's high time he learned," responded Leeyes instantly. "And," he added, "not only are there men in the Force who know everything about bullets in every shape and form, but my painful experience is that they'll all be dying to tell him. Take my advice, Sloan, and don't let them start talking to you about trajectories, or you'll never get your tea."

NOWADAYS news travels round the world with something approximating more to the speed of light than that of sound and, in the global village that the world has in consequence become, very little remains secret for long.

The first intelligence to reach the Sheikhdom of Lasserta from London did so very quickly indeed. It arrived well within the deadline set by Sheikh Ben Hajal Kisra for the sequestration of the Anglo-Lassertan Mineral Company's assets there, and it was to the effect that Alan Ottershaw would be coming back to face the music.

There had never been any embargo about telling it not in Gath or publishing it not in the streets of Askelon lest the daughters of the Philistines rejoice, so when Malcolm Forfar, the company's chief executive in Lasserta, heard the news at the firm's headquarters at the minehead at Wadeem, he promptly sped into Gatt-el-Abbas to talk to the Ambassador.

"I wonder what Ben Hajal Kirsa'll do now?" said Forfar without preamble. "Have a show trial, do ye think?"

Anthony Heber Hibbs waved the mine manager into a chair while his amiable wife Mollie (affectionately known throughout the entire British colony as the Diplomatic Bag) tactfully withdrew. "What will you have to drink?"

"What? Oh, a long Roman, please." Forfar was a hard-bitten Scot whose favourite tipple was Glen Morangie malt whisky, but he did not say so. Instead he exploded with: "Talk about brinkmanship!"

"Time, my dear fellow, is an ingredient of diplomacy," said the Ambassador. "One long Roman."

"Thank you." Forfar accepted the ice-cool drink of lime juice and soda water called "Roman" by the expatriate British on the strength of the ancient Latin tag about when being in Rome, doing as the Romans do. The consumption of alcohol was not permitted in the Sheikhdom of Lasserta.

"And timing," added Heber Hibbs, sitting down himself, "is one of the tools of the trade of diplomacy."

"I daresay it is," responded the mine manager warmly. He had spent most of the previous weekend devising ingenious ways to scuttle the mining works in the best *Graf Spee* tradition. "But, man, just waiting for orders is a gey hard business."

"Yes, indeed," agreed the Ambassador soothingly. His own instructions came direct from Whitehall and therefore he was not only accustomed to waiting for them but, by now, more or less reconciled to their ambiguity. Governments of every complexion always liked to keep all their options open for as long as possible.

And to have a scapegoat handy if things did not work out well.

Malcolm Forfar sank the lime-juice drink without relish and said,

"Do you know what I was supposed to do the minute we got to the Sheikh's deadline for Ottershaw's return?"

"Tell me," said Anthony Heber Hibbs, who had already heard the answer to this from sources euphemistically referred to as "close to Whitehall."

"Suspend production!" Forfar snorted, losing the panloaf Scots he usually spoke. "I ask ye, man! What guid in the world would suspending production do?"

"In itself, nothing," said the Ambassador. "As a gesture, I suspect quite a lot."

In the diplomatic world gestures had almost as great a significance as in the anthropological one. They had, it transpired, none at all in the engineering field.

"Cutting off your nose to spite your face, if you ask me," declared Forfar. "That's all that is. I can tell you, foregoing output never did a company any good." He paused and added, "Unless you're in diamonds, of course."

Neither, thought Heber Hibbs, did disagreeing with your ground landlord, but he did not say so. "Tell me," he said instead, "is suspending production technically very difficult?"

"Well, no," said Forfar grudgingly. "We have to do it from time to time anyway to check our shafts and lifting gear and so forth, but it's not good practice to do it when you don't have to. We work to some pretty tight schedules for some of our customers, I can tell you."

That the main purchaser of the ore containing queremitte mined by the Anglo-Lassertan Mineral Company was the Ministry of Defence Procurement was left unsaid by both men.

"This accident in which Ottershaw was involved," began Heber Hibbs again after a suitable interval.

"What about it?"

"I suppose you're sure it was an accident?" The Ambassador introduced a new train of thought at exactly the right moment, casually posing a question that had been put to him rather more urgently by Whitehall. And in code, too.

The engineer frowned. "You're not the only person who wants to know that."

"No?"

The engineer frowned. "For starters I've had the Defence Procurement people sniffing round asking the same question."

The Ambassador hadn't known that. "And?" he asked, since hors d'oeuvres was usually followed by a main course, "who else?"

"It was the first thing my firm wondered, too." Malcolm Forfar added with the supreme indifference of the engineer to wider affairs, "They've got a Parliamentary Select Committee on their tails. Did you know that?"

"Once they get going," said Heber Hibbs profoundly, "select committees sit on everyone's tails."

"They don't like the cost of queremitte," said Forfar simply.

"No. I can see that they might not." He reached for Forfar's empty glass. "Tell me, what did happen?"

Forfar shrugged his shoulders. "All I can tell you is what Ottershaw told me. He said that he was driving down towards the market here in Gatt-el-Abbas when this Lassertan fellow just stepped out in front of his car. Came out from behind a parked lorry without looking was what Ottershaw told me. Anyway," carried on Forfar, waving away the suggestion of another Roman drink, "he didn't have any warning or time to stop or anything. First thing Alan knew about it was this chap's head hitting his windscreen. He never had a chance."

"That," remarked the Ambassador drily, "would seem to have gone for both of them."

"You know what these Lassertans are like," said Malcolm Forfar. "They've got about as much road sense as hedgehogs."

Her Britannic Majesty's Ambassador concurred with a nod. The motor car had come late to Lasserta and then the Sheikhdom's road-traffic accident statistics demonstrated a touching faith in an afterlife. "What we don't know, Forfar," he said, "and what we may never know is something important about the victim."

The mine manager looked up.

"Did he fall," said Heber Hibbs slowly, "or was he pushed?"

FIVE

And Pain Has Exhausted Every Limb

THERE MIGHT HAVE BEEN no post-mortem examination of the body of the late Alan John Ottershaw: there certainly was one on the Camulos Society's portrayal of the Battle of Lewes. The Committee met in full session as soon as Alan Ottershaw's death and funeral were beginning to recede in public memory. The Secretary had just managed not to refer to a death in action when making his report—but it had been a near thing.

"Sorry I'm late," said Adrian Dungey, the veterinary surgeon, sliding into his seat after the Committee meeting had started. "I had an emergency call to Toad Hall."

"Batrachomyomachy broken out?" suggested Bertram Rauly.

"That sounds nasty," said a Committee man.

"Is it infectious?" asked somebody else. "Like foot and mouth?"

Adrian Dungey gave a light laugh. "Nothing like that I'm happy to say. Batrachomyomachy was a battle between frogs and mice, wasn't it, sir?"

Bertram Rauly nodded. "It's one of those things that the Greeks had a word for."

"Would the battle do for the Camulos Society?" asked the Secretary. "Not that we're short of ideas," he added hastily.

"We wouldn't need an armourer, Adrian, for a battle between frogs and mice, would we?" said the Treasurer. Adrian Dungey, good with his hands, acted as the Society's armourer at battles calling for metal weaponry. "I'm afraid I haven't had the benefit of a classical education, you see."

The young man smiled. "I daresay toothpicks would do. Shall we call the Frog general Jeremy Fisher?"

"As long as you don't call him Pétain," growled Bertram Rauly, who had escaped from the beaches of Dunkirk by the skin of his teeth.

"And the Mouse one Field Marshal Michael . . ."

"Before we get on to our next battle," said the Chairman importantly, "there are one or two little matters arising out of the last one to be cleared up."

It was some little time before these were disposed of and the Secretary could move on to the correspondence.

"I've had a letter," he announced, "from the University of Calleshire—well, from an undergraduate there, actually. His name is Richard Godstone and he's at Almstone College at the University." The Secretary waved the sheet of paper in his hand at the Committee members. "It says here that he and his friends want to know if the Camulos Society would consider having a re-enactment of Guy Fawkes attempting to blow up the Houses of Parliament."

"No battle there," objected a purist.

"Somebody shopped him, didn't they?" said another member immediately. "Lost their nerve at the last minute and turned him in."

"Not a lot of action in either case, was there?" objected the Treasurer, dismissing thus one of the most fraught periods of English history.

"A late autumn meeting would be quite an idea, though," mused the Secretary. "And a bonfire for the children."

"The bonfire," pointed out Bertram Rauly astringently, "was for Parliament."

"And fireworks," said the Secretary. His two sons liked fireworks.

Major Puiver's response was even more pertinent. "What's in it for them? The students, I mean."

"There's no such thing as a free lunch," concurred the Chairman sagely.

The Secretary turned the page over. "They say they're making a study of Parliament and some of its members."

"So did Guy Fawkes," said Adrian Dungey, "didn't he?"

"And they would like to participate in a full-scale and historically accurate reconstruction of the episode."

"Episode!" snorted the Major. "That's a fine way of describing one of the——"

"They tortured Guy Fawkes, didn't they?" intervened the purist with all the detachment that some three hundred years and more could bring.

"If they're looking for old cellars," drawled Rauly, "and I daresay they are, they can use the old Motte."

"Provided they don't blow it up, of course," added the Treasurer. Getting insurance cover for the Camulos Society had not been easy.

"Or knock it down," said Adrian Dungey. "Did you hear about the piece of stone that came down during the re-enactment? It just missed the Member."

"That's being looked into," replied Bertram Rauly rather shortly. "By the way, was anything unusual found on the field of battle afterwards?"

"How unusual?" enquired the Chairman. "Somebody left a cross-bow out in the long grass."

"Chicken-bones," said Rauly unexpectedly.

"But, Bertram, we had pheasant for luncheon."

"Exactly."

HER MAJESTY'S CORONER for East Calleshire, Mr. David Locombe-Stapleford, was a solicitor in late middle-age to whom the epithet "crusty" might truly be applied.

He was almost archetypal in appearance and in manner, having inherited both the appointment to the office of Coroner and a long-established legal practice in the town of Berebury from his father. The archaic electrical fittings in his office in the town stemmed from Mr. Locombe-Stapleford's grandfather's time, but the roll-top desk and the chairs into which he waved Detective Inspector Sloan and Detective Constable Crosby were from an earlier epoch still.

The Coroner was an autocrat of the old school and was afraid of nothing and nobody. Except, it presently transpired, of creating a precedent.

"If I understand you correctly, Inspector," he said, adjusting his glasses, "you are asking me to enquire into some ashes."

"That is so, sir." Sloan hadn't sat on a black horse-hair chair for a long time and was surprised all over again at how uncomfortable he found it.

"It is a misdemeanour," said the old solicitor sternly, "to prevent the holding of an inquest, which ought to be held, by disposing of the body. *Price,* Queen's Bench Division, 1884."

"Yes, sir. Quite so." Detective Inspector Sloan wasn't really concerned about simple misdemeanours. He had something quite different in mind. "It isn't exactly——"

"And, in any case, Inspector, a body is no longer a *sine qua non* for an inquest."

"No," agreed Sloan hastily, before the Coroner started rummaging about in his memory for when that had become the rule.

"A presumption," he continued frostily, "that there has been a body is quite sufficient for the law to act."

"Yes, sir, I am aware of——"

"There is, in any case, often evidence that a body has existed," rumbled on the Coroner, "which may not now be present."

Detective Constable Crosby, who didn't like flying, said unexpectedly, "A name on a passenger list."

Sloan hadn't even realised that the Detective Constable had been listening: he didn't usually.

"After one of the atomic bombs had exploded, gentlemen, there was just a shadow of a man on the ground where he had been standing." Mr. David Locombe-Stapleford had never entered an aircraft and had no intention of doing so, but he was accustomed to keeping ahead of detective constables.

"The Turin Shroud," contributed Detective Inspector Sloan, whose mother was a great churchwoman.

"The Motorway Man." Mr. Locombe-Stapleford could cap detective inspectors, too, with ease. "No doubt you remember the case, Inspector? My confrère over at Luston only had a hole to go on."

"A man-shaped and a man-sized hole," responded Sloan, a trifle stiffly. His own opposite number in the Luston Division had come in for a good deal of ribbing about the Motorway Man. It had taken a lot of valuable police time and energy to consign Luston's Motorway Man into the same generic category, so to speak, as the Piltdown one.

"A hoax, nevertheless," said the Coroner severely, "perpetrated by those who ought to have known better."

"They made a mould which disintegrated without trace after the concrete was set, didn't they?" said Detective Constable Crosby chattily, his wayward interest momentarily diverted by the sight of Mr. Locombe-Stapleford pulling down an antiquated electric light with a green glass shade. It worked from a white porcelain pulley and counterweight suspended from the ceiling. And it resembled nothing so much as an artifact in the office of a sheriff in a Spaghetti Western.

"So, Inspector," said the Coroner, centering the lamp over his desk, "you are inviting me to enquire into some ashes, or, rather, the death to which they relate?"

"Yes, sir."

"And you wish to prevent their return to the deceased's relatives?"

"Not so much prevent," said Sloan cautiously, "as delay."

"Interfere with their disposition, then," amended the solicitor. "I take it that what you want is to obstruct the crematorium authorities' normal procedure?"

"I have reason to believe, sir, that the death certification in this case might not have been totally accurate."

"I am reliably informed, Inspector," Mr. Locombe-Stapleford said with some acidity, "that the same thing might be said of approximately half of all cases where the cause of death is based on clinical information alone——"

Detective Constable Crosby leaned forward with interest. "How do they kn——"

"—where there has subsequently been a post-mortem examination," finished the Coroner triumphantly.

"There wasn't an autopsy in this case," said Detective Inspector Sloan with commendable restraint. "I understand that the certifying doctors were satisfied that the deceased died from heart failure."

"At least," sniffed Mr. Locombe-Stapleford, "they don't appear to have belonged to the 'give it a long name and nobody will ask any questions' school of medicine, do they, Inspector?"

"I couldn't say, sir, I'm sure," said Sloan austerely. "All I can say is that I am advised by the Regional Forensic Science Laboratory that a metal pellet said to have been found in the deceased's ashes at cremation was of recent manufacture and had not been in the body long enough for oxidisation to have taken place."

The Coroner brought the rise-and-fall electric fitment down as far as it would go, the better to concentrate its light on a sheet of paper in the middle of his blotting pad. "What I need to know, Inspector," he said, "is whether this death has given rise to a reasonable doubt in your mind or anyone else's about the cause of death."

"Yes," said Sloan simply, adding, "although at this stage unfortunately we do not know whether or not the pellet had any bearing on the death."

"Gunshot wound?" The Coroner was of a vintage to know what the letters "g.s.w." stood for.

"Not exactly, sir, although it might have been shot with a gun."

"Umbrella jab?" The Coroner was obviously more up to date than he seemed.

"Too soon to say."

Mr. Locombe-Stapleford unscrewed the cap of an old-fashioned fountain pen. "Which is why you wish to—er—postpone the proposed inhumation of the ashes?"

"Yes, sir."

"And why you wish me, Inspector, acting in my capacity as Coroner, to order an autopsy?"

"An examination of such remains as there are," qualified Sloan.

"I see." Mr. Locombe-Stapleford looked shrewdly at the policeman over the top of his glasses.

By nothing more than a whisker Sloan avoided a natural tendency to say "please" inculcated in him at a very early age by a mother who placed a high value on the word. Instead he waited in what he trusted was a courteous silence as the Coroner rumbled on.

"While you," said Mr. Locombe-Stapleford, "investigate a death after a duly certified cremation has taken place."

"Yes, sir," said Sloan. Never apologise and never explain was what Benjamin Disraeli had advised. Prime Ministers, it seemed, were strong on advice.

"H'm." Mr. Locombe-Stapleford's pen hovered over the sheet of paper on his blotting pad. "Give me the deceased's name and last-known address."

"Alan John Ottershaw," complied Detective Inspector Sloan, "of

April Cottage, High Street, Mellamby, but he'd only just got home from abroad."

He wished he hadn't mentioned the fact. If there was one matter on which all the coroners he had ever known were equally sensitive to, it was whether or not a body lay within their jurisdiction.

"Abroad?" barked the Coroner, immediately laying down his pen. His writ ran no further than halfway across the county of Calleshire.

"The Middle East," Sloan answered him, equally unhappily. "The Sheikhdom of Lasserta, to be precise."

Mr. Locombe-Stapleford frowned. "So this—er—pellet could have been—er—introduced into the body of this man while it was not in England?"

"Yes, sir," said Sloan. As far as the Coroner was concerned the phrase "not in England" was probably the ultimate in every sense. In sentiment it might have come straight from John of Gaunt's "sceptr'd isle" speech. Or Robert Browning's "Oh, to be in England now that April's there."

"Such a circumstance," said Mr. David Locombe-Stapleford severely, "could make for difficulties."

"Yes, sir," said Sloan. "There is something else, too . . ."

"They look upon sudden death quite differently abroad," the Coroner swept on.

That, thought Sloan to himself, was pure Kipling if anything was.

"Quite differently," repeated the Coroner.

The lesser breeds without the law, was how that poet had put it: Sloan wondered if the Superintendent knew that.

"And hot countries have other customs, anyway," said the Coroner unspecifically.

Sloan nodded, forbearing to mention sky burial.

"But not so many procedures," said Mr. Locombe-Stapleford, reaching for another form with evident satisfaction.

"No, sir." Sloan was with him there. Any country whose procedure for burial at sea required the Ministry of Agriculture, Fisheries and Food to be notified under the Dumping at Sea Act 1974 was not short on attention to detail.

He ventured to say so to the Coroner: and regretted it immediately.

"That Act, Inspector," came the precise response, "only applies within the three-mile territorial limit."

Sloan might have known. It was the "not in England" syndrome all over again beyond those three important miles.

"The position outside territorial waters," said the Coroner, "is less certain."

The silver sea in which this sceptr'd isle was set, thought Sloan irreverently, wasn't entirely covered by the Dumping at Sea Act, then.

"But," said the Coroner, "the Removal of Bodies Regulations 1954 probably apply."

"No good dying on board ship, either, then, is it?" remarked Detective Constable Crosby cheerfully.

"Ah," responded the Coroner alertly, "dying on board ship is, paradoxically, quite a different matter."

Sloan waited.

"Then, the body can be disposed of as part of the normal working of the ship."

"Well, I never!" said Detective Constable Crosby, while Sloan had almost come round to the view that there was something to be said for sky burial after all.

The Detective Inspector returned to the matter in hand. "As I was saying, sir, there is something else."

"Well, Inspector, what is it?" The Coroner looked up, pushing the task light to one side.

"This pellet that has been found in the remains . . ."

"What about it?"

"It's made of queremitte."

"Queremitte?" The Coroner's general knowledge wasn't as good as that of Superintendent Leeyes.

Detective Constable Crosby repeated, parrot-fashion, something he had only just learned. "Queremitte is a very hard metal which is the principal export of the Sheikhdom of Lasserta."

SIX

When the Will Has Forgotten the Life-Long Aim

APRIL COTTAGE was set in the middle of the High Street at Mellamby and was not far from the parish church of St. Martin's. It was Mellamby Motte, though, that still dominated the view. The de Caqueville family, the builders of the earliest castle at Mellamby, had chosen their site well, and its remains—only the original keep was standing now, the bailey having been spoiled long ago—caught the eye from all over the village of Mellamby.

On the working principle that time spent on reconnaissance was seldom wasted, Detective Inspector Sloan and Detective Constable Crosby had had a word with the local village bobby before calling on Alan Ottershaw's widow.

"She's called Hazel," said Police Constable Colin Turton, "and she's a local girl. Old Rebble, the vet's daughter, actually. She's got a by-name, too, in the village."

Sloan leaned forward attentively. They had habitual criminals with nicknames which gave a clue to the characteristics of the person. Mrs. Gasmeter Bradley, for instance, specialised in just one thing.

Constable Turton frowned. "They call her 'Hamamelis' or something like that."

"Witch-hazel," translated Detective Inspector Sloan, quondam gardener.

"Oh, I remember." Constable Turton's face cleared. "The stuff they used to rub on bruises." He hesitated. "Or was that arnica?"

Detective Constable Crosby wasn't interested in homely remedies. "What's she like?" he asked.

"Hazel Ottershaw?" Turton raised his eyebrows expressively. "Good-looking. Stylish, too. Mind you, there's never been any shortage of money in that outfit."

"That helps," said Crosby. "Great stuff, money."

Sloan wasn't so sure about that, but this was no time for debate. "Go on."

"As well," Turton said, "as being married to a mining engineer who can't have been doing too badly, thank you, her father is the senior partner of the biggest veterinary practice in this part of the world."

"Why," asked Sloan, with an eye for essentials, "wasn't she out in Lasserta with her husband?"

"Couldn't stand the heat," said the village policeman, "or so I hear. And then they had two babies in quick succession. I gather this place her husband was stationed at—Wadi something or other—was no place for small children."

April Cottage, Mellamby, Calleshire, on the other hand, it presently transpired, was a good place for small children.

"My mother lives just up the road, you see," explained Mrs. Hazel Ottershaw to the two detectives. She was indeed a good-looking girl, with as good a pair of ankles as Sloan had seen in many a long day and the fine, semi-translucent skin which usually went with freckles. "She's been a great help with Julian and Kate . . ." Her voice faltered. "I really don't know what I should have done without her."

"No, madam. Quite so."

"When you telephoned, Inspector, I asked her to come down so that there would be someone to look after them while you were here." Her face clouded. "They don't understand, you see. They're too young, poor little lambs."

"No, madam. Naturally they don't." Detective Inspector Sloan was using this form of address advisedly, although Hazel Ottershaw couldn't have been all that far on in her twenties. In his view, grief and a decent formality went together: there was a certain dignity to be observed in proper mourning, and an instinctive unapproachability.

Hazel Ottershaw's responses were almost rigidly studied and polite, too. "I'm afraid they're not going to remember their father either, Inspector," she said in a voice that was slightly shaky. "They're too young. It's very sad, isn't it?"

"Yes, madam."

They had found Hazel Ottershaw sitting alone in a room with the blinds half down. Those shafts of sunlight that were streaming into April Cottage were full of dancing dust-motes and there was about the place the stillness and inanition that customarily follow a bereavement. Detective Constable Crosby hadn't liked the half-dark and had audibly stubbed his toe on a reproduction Pembroke table.

"What makes it worse, Inspector," she continued, her tightly controlled speech beginning to relax a little, "is that Julian at least had got quite used to Alan coming and going."

"Quite so, madam," he said. Hazel Ottershaw was not to know that Detective Inspector Sloan welcomed her use of her husband's name as a good sign. Death, like birth, came to half a million homes a year in the United Kingdom. It was a statistic which often got forgotten, even by policemen, but reaction to the event did tend to follow a pattern and the ability of those to whom the deceased had been near and dear to refer to him or her by name was an important milestone in bereavement.

They were too late, all the same, noted the policeman in Sloan automatically, to observe a physical manifestation—the rocking motion of profound grief—which crossed every cultural barrier the world over.

Hazel Ottershaw visibly braced herself to look him full in the face and said starkly, "Only there isn't going to be any more coming ever again after this going, is there?"

"No, madam, I'm afraid not."

"And the children aren't going to understand."

"No." Sloan's own responses were equally stark. It was part of his own personal credo that widows should be steered away from fools' paradises. "I trust, madam, that you won't have to move house or anything like that, will you?" If there was one thing in his experience that compounded the grief of the recently widowed it was moving house while still in a state of shock.

"No," she shook her head quickly. "That's one great blessing, I can see that, and I'm very thankful. April Cottage is ours—I mean, mine. It was a wedding present from my father. His assistant vets always used to live here until Alan and I got married. Now, they have to find lodgings——" She turned her head sharply as an older woman came through the door. "Ah, Inspector, this is my mother."

Mrs. Rebble was a plump, comfortable-looking woman. She was carrying one child in her arms as she came into the room and had another clutching at her skirt. She also appeared to be accomplishing the difficult double-act required of those close to the recently bereaved of both sharing their distress and being practical too. She pointed to the half-drawn curtains. "Darling, do you think we could have just a little more light? The poor gentlemen won't be able to see what they're writing."

"Thank you," said Sloan politely.

Detective Constable Crosby, whose big toe was still hurting after its encounter with the table, regrettably saw fit to say under his breath, "She should have the light so she can see to tell the truth."

Sloan, promising himself that he would deal with Crosby later, hoped that neither Hazel Ottershaw nor her mother had heard him.

"Stay with Mummy, darlings," Mrs. Rebble said to the children, "while Granny brings in some tea."

Detective Constable Crosby almost fell over himself in being helpful with the tea-tray. Whatever strange ambition had drawn him into the police force, it wasn't to run the risk of being a child-minder.

"Julian has been as good as gold in the kitchen," remarked Mrs. Rebble, returning with a large pot of tea. Crosby followed with a jug of hot water like a vice-regal train bearer. "He's been playing with some Plasticine."

Sloan, who would never be able to equate goodness with Plasticine, accepted a cup of tea and came back to the matter in hand. "As I explained on the telephone, madam," he said to Hazel Ottershaw, "we're just checking up on your husband's sudden death."

"Because he'd been abroad such a lot?" she asked.

"In a way," said Sloan evasively. "Can you tell me anything about his last visit home?"

"I wasn't expecting him," said Hazel Ottershaw, releasing her hold on her small son. "He arrived home quite out of the blue late on the Friday night by the last train. He told me he'd only just caught that by the skin of his teeth and hadn't had time to ring me or anything like that."

"He wasn't due back?"

She shook her head. "Not for ages."

"It wasn't so long since we'd all said goodbye to him," contributed Mrs. Rebble, proffering a bowl of sugar to the two policemen. "That was when he went back to Lasserta after his last leave. I was so surprised to see him myself in the village on the Saturday morning."

"The first thing I knew about Alan being back in England at all," said Hazel Ottershaw dully, "was when I heard his latch-key in the door. It was very late and I was in bed."

"He'd never come home like that before? Without warning, I mean."

"Never." She ran a hand over her face as if to brush away a memory. "I've always known when to expect him in the past. He's either written or cabled without fail."

"But not this time?" said Sloan. Changes in a pattern were always interesting to a detective.

"Not this time, Inspector." Mrs. Hazel Ottershaw's teacup rattled ever so slightly in its saucer. "It wasn't ordinary leave, you see. Something had gone wrong at work, he said. Very wrong."

"Ah," said Sloan encouragingly. He couldn't think for the moment of what the Middle Eastern equivalent of "trouble at t'mill" was likely to be: but there would be one.

"He hadn't got the sack or anything like that," she added swiftly.

Alan Ottershaw's mother-in-law said in stout tones, "Of course not, darling."

"But he didn't want to tell me what the trouble was," said Hazel Ottershaw.

"He didn't want to worry you," said Mrs. Rebble.

"All he wanted to do," said Alan Ottershaw's widow evenly, "was to get on to his Member of Parliament as fast as possible."

"I see." Detective Inspector Sloan made a note. In his experience, people usually only wanted to get on to their Members of Parliament when they wished to complain about their alleged ill-usage at the hands of civil servants, local government officers, and other unfortunate administrators.

"Luckily he managed to arrange to talk to Peter Corbishley after the Garden Meeting at Mellamby Place on the Saturday afternoon," said Hazel Ottershaw. "He told me after that he felt a whole lot happier."

"Happier?" In Sloan's book Members of Parliament were seldom renowned as bringers of joy.

"He knew then what his rights were."

Sloan nodded at that. Knowing where one stood was always important. He said, "Do you know in what connection he was reassured, madam?"

"Extradition back to Lasserta from the United Kingdom," replied Hazel Ottershaw, adding bleakly, "although as it happened he needn't have worried, need he?"

So, thought Sloan to himself, it had been a case of being "not in England" after all. He did not say so though, but asked instead, "Was your husband at all unwell when he came home?"

She hesitated. "The doctors kept asking me that. He was very, very tired when he got back and a bit jet-lagged, but he said his main trouble was that he couldn't sleep in spite of being flaked out."

"He was all right on the Sunday morning first thing," said Mrs. Rebble, "because he stood in for poor Mr. Rauly and got killed instead of him."

"Really, madam?" said Sloan politely. They'd stopped teaching the story of Damon and Phythias in schools these days, but it had featured in the curriculum when Sloan had been a lad.

"Mr. Rauly had sprained his ankle on the Saturday evening after the Garden Meeting," explained Hazel Ottershaw, "and so he couldn't take part in the Battle of Lewes that was staged here on the Sunday."

"Ah, I see." He now realised that distant rumblings of the reenactment of the battle had been audible in the Police Station canteen at Berebury. They had emanated from Inspector Harpe of the Traffic Division. Inspector Harpe—known as Happy Harry because he had never been known to smile—had had a great deal to say on the subjects of medieval conflicts, narrow country lanes, and modern motorists.

"Alan happened to be there on the spot at Mellamby Place on the Sunday morning," said Hazel Ottershaw, "with me——"

"Hazel was a beautiful Queen Eleanor," put in Hazel's mother. "She looked lovely in a kirtle."

"—and without a role," said Hazel, "because, of course, nobody knew he was going to be back here in Mellamby at the time of the re-enactment."

"Of course," murmured Sloan.

"Green has always suited Hazel," said Mrs. Rebble fondly, "and those old-fashioned head-dresses are very stylish."

"So," said Hazel Ottershaw rather desperately, "Alan played the part which Mr. Rauly had been going to take."

"And he wasn't ill on the Sunday morning, I can assure you," said Mrs. Rebble warmly. "He fought like a Trojan all morning. I saw him myself. I shall never forget the great fight he had with the King —that was Adrian Dungey really. And Adrian was good, too. He's one of my husband's junior partners, you know. Their fight was marvellous to watch."

Detective Constable Crosby brightened visibly at the mention of fighting, his wandering attention engaged at last. "Who was he being?"

"William de Wilton," said Mrs. Rebble, the light of battle clearly still in her eye. "He had to be killed before luncheon, you know."

This last was too much for Hazel Ottershaw.

Her self-control snapped suddenly. She burst into tears and fled from the room.

"You want me to examine what, Inspector?" asked Dr. Dabbe. The consultant pathologist was sitting at his desk in his office attached to the mortuary at Berebury District General Hospital.

"Some human ashes, Doctor," said Sloan. He and young Detective Constable Crosby were sitting opposite the pathologist, who seemed to be in one of his merrier moods.

"That's what I thought you said," replied Dr. Dabbe. "Well, if it's those pesky archaeologists excavating outside the old Roman wall down by the river again, I should tell them to——"

"It isn't, Doctor."

"They're always coming up with cinerary urns full of ashes."

"Are they?" Detective Inspector Sloan seized on this as a beginning. "And what exactly can you tell from them, Doctor?"

"That there's been a cremation burial," said the pathologist jovially.

"And anything else?"

Dr. Dabbe hitched a shoulder. "Precious little."

"Pity, that."

"Not nothing at all, of course. I'm not saying that, Sloan. There's always something to be got even from, as the poet put it so well 'A handful of grey ashes, long long ago at rest.' "

"Good." It would be going against the grain for the doctor, anyway, to admit defeat: Sloan knew that. Sooner or later professional pride would rear its ugly head and an opinion would be offered.

"Well, if there's a fragment of femur shaft you can sometimes have a view of the sex of the deceased." He grinned. "Although, unless it's in the region of the *linea aspera,* I must say it's pretty nearly as difficult as doing day-old chicks."

Sloan said austerely, "The sex does not present any difficulty."

"And," continued the doctor, "if there are clear remains of two bones of which *homo sapiens* has only one—the sacrum of the Atlas vertebra, for instance—then the presence in the ashes of at least two individuals will have been demonstrated." He paused and added gravely, "I think, Sloan, even a jury would agree with that—if you're going in for juries, that is."

"I'm sure they would, Doctor," responded Sloan with matching solemnity, although you never knew with juries. "Actually, in this case——"

"Stands to reason," contributed Detective Constable Crosby. "Doesn't it?"

"Yes, indeed," said the pathologist hastily. "The same applies if they weigh more than—say—nine hundred grammes. Of course, the archaeologists can also deduce a good deal from what was buried with the body."

"So, I hope," said Sloan piously, "can detectives."

"And grave goods," continued Dr. Dabbe, "often make it possible to distinguish between the centuries."

"I think you might say," murmured Sloan, "that, in a manner of speaking, it is the grave goods which are our problem."

The pathologist leaned forward. "Tell me, Sloan, do they need to know if it was the noblest Roman of them all, then?"

"Not exactly, Doctor."

Dr. Dabbe cocked his head alertly. "Say on, Inspector. This sounds interesting."

"We were hoping," said Sloan, "that something more than—er—just the fact of cremation might perhaps be determinable."

"Teeth can tell you a lot," offered Dabbe, "if you're lucky."

"It's not the teeth we're interested in," said Sloan. "At least, I don't think so."

"The provenance can be helpful," said Dr. Dabbe briskly. "Archaeology and forensic medicine have a lot in common, you know."

Sloan cleared his throat. "Not in this case, Doctor. At least, I don't think so."

"The urn and strata can often yield valuable information, too."

"They aren't really relevant——"

"And," said the doctor, warming to his theme, "you can sometimes calculate the length of time that they have been buried by——"

"These haven't been buried, Doctor," said Sloan gently.

"Yet," added Detective Constable Crosby, who had had the full history of the ashes explained to him in the car on the way from the Police Station to Mrs. Ottershaw's house at Mellamby.

The pathologist began to look very attentive. "So, Sloan, if I were to tell you that sometimes the charcoal fragments can be a source of radio-carbon dating, you wouldn't be too excited?"

"No, Doctor."

"But if I were to tell you that there were some poisons, especially the heavy metals—thallium, for instance—which did survive the cremation process, you would be interested?"

"Very."

"Intriguing."

"Yes, Doctor." Detective Inspector Sloan launched into an explanation of the metal pellet found in the ashes that the crematorium had handed to Tod Morton, and which the young undertaker had accidentally spilt.

"It's not made of the alloy Vitallium, then," said the doctor. "The orthopods use that a lot but it's non-magnetic."

"No, not that."

"And it's not from a pace-maker."

"Oh?" Sloan looked up.

"They explode in the cremator," said Dr. Dabbe matter-of-factly, "if you leave 'em in. So you don't."

"The metallurgists," said Sloan, "report that the pellet found in Alan Ottershaw's ashes is modern, made of queremitte, and started life hollow—don't ask me how they know."

"They do it with mirrors," said Dabbe drily.

"It's a little misshapen now but they think it could have contained something."

"Go on, Sloan." The attention of the pathologist was fully engaged now. "I'm all ears."

"The ballistics people can't say whether it's been fired from a weapon but don't ask me how they know that either."

"And you, Sloan—stop me if I'm wrong—want me to say if it—or what might have been in it—could have been or contributed towards the cause of death? Right?"

"Right," said Sloan gratefully.

"And you want me to perform this feat from the ashes?"

"And the medical history."

Detective Constable Crosby leaned forward and contributed his mite. "It's not a lot, is it, doctor?"

"Oh, I don't know," said the pathologist equably. "There might have been less."

Crosby looked distinctly doubtful.

"Most men leave something behind them when they go," said the doctor.

Sloan said he was sure he hoped so, although to live in the minds of those they left behind was the most that some could manage.

"Even," said Dr. Dabbe, "if it's only what the poet called 'a richer earth.' Do you know your Rupert Brooke, gentlemen? We might only have had back, as he put it so well, the thoughts by England given."

"Can't have much less than that, can you?" agreed Crosby.

"Instead of a whole urnful of ashes," finished Dabbe.

"What we need to know, Doctor——" began Sloan, handing over a plastic exhibit bag.

"Among other things," interjected Detective Constable Crosby unnecessarily.

"—is whether a man would have felt something of the size of this little pellet going through his skin.

The pathologist frowned at the piece of metal. "It depends on what he was doing at the time and where it hit him."

"He might, he just might," advanced Sloan with caution, "have been taking part in a mock fight."

"Then," said the doctor immediately, "he may never have felt a thing."

Detective Inspector Sloan explained about the re-enactment.

"The Battle of Lewes?" echoed Dr. Dabbe. "That was good old Simon de Montfort and that tiresome King Henry III with the ptosis, wasn't it?"

"Ptosis, Doctor?"

"King Henry III had a droopy eyelid, Sloan." The doctor grimaced. "He was a real menace. In *The Divine Comedy*, Dante put him in the Third Circle of Hell for negligence, and quite right, too."

It was a new view of history to Sloan.

"Pity de Montfort didn't kill him, then and there," said the doctor, "except that I suppose we wouldn't have had the Westminster Abbey we have now and that would have been a pity, wouldn't it?"

"Yes, Doctor," said Sloan, adding manfully, "About these ashes . . ."

"Send them round, Sloan, send them round." The pathologist rubbed his hands. "I haven't had anything more interesting than an afternoon death for days now."

The policeman jerked his head interrogatively. Sloan had come across a lot of deaths in his time, but afternoon ones were new to him and he said so now to the pathologist.

"Of course they're new, Sloan," responded Dr. Dabbe. "To paraphrase the immortal John Webster, 'Death now has ten thousand and one several doors.'"

"I see," said Sloan, although he didn't. "Perhaps you would . . ."

"The Intensive Care outfit at the hospital double-checks the patients on life-support machines in the morning," amplified the doctor obligingly, "and if the recorders are still flat, then they triple-check them in the afternoon."

"And?"

"And if the lines are still flat." Dr. Dabbe waved his hands in an age-old gesture. "Then . . ."

"Then they pull the plug out," finished the Detective Constable for him, adding with chilling simplicity, "before tea."

SEVEN

And the Mind Can Only Disgrace Its Fame

THE MEMBER OF PARLIAMENT for the East Berebury Division of the County of Calleshire projected nothing but helpfulness to the two policemen who visited him at his constituency headquarters in the town.

He did it so well that Detective Inspector Sloan reminded himself that the very posture was probably part of the politician's stock-in-trade. Peter Corbishley was holding his head at a slightly sideways angle, supported by two fingers of his left hand, and conveying a faintly quizzical attitude that was meant to demonstrate an alert interest without commitment. As it happened it was a position he assumed almost daily in Parliament while listening to debate—and at weekends while trying to sort out the difficulties of his constituents.

"Ottershaw had problems all right, Inspector," he said when he had heard the policemen out. "Or, more precisely, his employers did." Peter Corbishley gave Sloan and Crosby a cogent résumé of the situation facing the Anglo-Lassertan Mineral Company after Ottershaw's road traffic accident. "Alan Ottershaw, poor fellow, had simply become a pawn in a power game overnight—and he knew it."

"In an international power game?" ventured Sloan, liking the idea as little as the Coroner had done.

"In a power game with very high stakes," said the Member, adding obliquely, "I daresay you know by now—you don't have to tell me, Inspector—that you know as much about our need for queremitte as I do."

Detective Inspector Sloan couldn't play the game of chess, but he did know how the pieces moved. "A pawn is the only piece on the board that can't move backwards, isn't it, sir?"

"What? Oh yes, Inspector, that's true. Very true. I'm sure Ottershaw would have put the clock to where it had been before he knocked the Lassertan down if he possibly could have done. However——"

"Yes?"

"I promised Ottershaw I would take up with the Home Office first thing on the Monday morning the important question of whether or not he could be extradited by the Lassertans." He frowned. "I'm afraid I couldn't tell the unfortunate chap then and there at the Garden Meeting exactly what sort of mutual arrangements we had with the Sheikhdom just like that."

"Quite so," said Sloan, who let the Police Manual do a lot of his own remembering of legal detail for him.

"I didn't even know at the time whether we had an extradition treaty with the Lassertans at all—let alone whether it was a convention or simply a declaration—not off the cuff."

"I see, sir." There had been a difference between a felony and a misdemeanour which those who were not of the Law found difficult to comprehend.

"Or even a protocol," continued the Member. He coughed. "I did, though, manage to have a word with one of the Parliamentary Under-Secretaries at the Foreign Office——"

"Ah," said Sloan encouragingly.

"—about the Anglo-Lassertan Mineral Company's position." A new thought appeared to strike the politician. "It's just as well, Inspector, that Parliament is in recess just now."

"Just as well," agreed Sloan, who was a member of a round-the-clock, round-the-calendar Force. "And what about the company's position?"

"Tricky," said Corbishley. "Very tricky."

Sloan wasn't surprised to hear it.

"It's the queremitte that makes the difference, of course," said the Member.

Sloan wasn't altogether surprised to hear that either. He'd already established that queremitte was what Winston Churchill would have called "one of the sinews of war." "We thought it might," he said. This was generous of him since Crosby did not appear to have thought at all.

The Member lowered his eyes a fraction: a sign well known to interrogation experts. "It seems, Inspector, that there might be more to the whole business than meets the eye."

"There often is," said Sloan prosaically, forbearing to add anything about what the eye didn't see, the heart didn't grieve over. This was never the police view. "Tell me."

"The Parliamentary Select Committee looking into the cost to the Ministry of Defence Procurement of queremitte is—er—setting up a lot of waves just now."

"Anglo-Lassertan taking them for a ride, are they?" asked Detective Constable Crosby with interest.

The politician's response was professionally tempered. "It was when the Foreign Office chappie started talking about keeping the Ministry of Defence Procurement in the picture over Ottershaw's problems," said Peter Corbishley, "that I began to realise that matters might just get out of hand very quickly."

"If Ottershaw hadn't died, you mean?" said Sloan in the tones of one anxious to get everything clear.

"I didn't know then that he had," said Peter Corbishley with apparent frankness. "One way and another I spent most of the Monday in London talking about his predicament, which naturally I wouldn't have done had I known about his having died from a heart attack."

"Naturally," said Sloan.

"I left Ottershaw to spend the Monday sorting out with his solicitor exactly what his employers—as employers, you understand—could make him do."

"And what they could do to him if he didn't," added Sloan. Nearly everyone forgot that in legal matters it took two to tango.

"What's that? Oh, yes, of course, Inspector. Well, as I said, I left him to talk to the lawyers about his situation while I applied myself to seeing how far the Lassertans could go. I didn't see him at all on the Sunday—I understand he had been—er—conscripted into taking part in the battle——"

"As William de Wilton," rejoined Sloan solemnly.

"—and until David Chadwick—he's my Agent—telephoned me and told me the news, that's what I thought Alan Ottershaw would be about on the Monday."

"Kicked the bucket by then, hadn't he?" said Crosby from the sidelines.

"Both the Lassertans and his employers," observed Sloan with speed, "would appear to have had some kind of vested interest in making a human sacrifice out of Ottershaw."

"Just as well he was saved by the bell, then, wasn't it?" remarked Crosby brightly. "If there is a fate worse than death, that is."

"Well . . ." temporised Peter Corbishley. The politician was too experienced to make an immediate comment, while Sloan made a mental note to explain to the Detective Constable the difference between a bell and a knell.

"If," said Detective Inspector Sloan equally carefully, "Lasserta didn't happen to have this valuable seam of queremitte ore . . ."

"Ah," said Corbishley, sitting up very straight, "that would be different. Then I don't suppose anyone would give you more than a handful of dates for it. There isn't any oil there, if that's what you mean."

"What about strategic importance?" As far as Sloan was concerned this wasn't as easy to calculate now that the map was no longer coloured pink somewhere on nearly every page in every atlas.

The Member of Parliament gave a hollow laugh. "In that part of the world, Inspector, who can say? Your guess would be as good as mine and we'd both probably be wrong."

Sloan cleared his throat. "Middle Eastern politics—"

"Are like the Schleswig-Holstein Question, Inspector."

"Sir?"

"There are only three men who have ever understood that."

"Really, sir?"

"One was Prince Albert, who was dead."

"Like Queen Anne?" ventured Sloan tentatively, since it seemed a historical matter.

"The second," swept on Corbishley, not listening, "was a German professor who became mad."

"Ah." It was the most non-committal sound Sloan could make.

"And the third was Lord Palmerston."

"Indeed, sir?"

"And he had forgotten."

Detective Inspector Sloan brought the conversation firmly back to the realms of England and the present. "I understand, sir, that you yourself had been subjected to some harassment at Mellamby that weekend."

"That's what 'Government of the people, by the people, for the people' means, Inspector," said the Member, relaxing. "It made a change from having wholesale disruption from the University students at Berebury Town Hall, like last year."

"You had a heckler." The fracas at the Town Hall last year had been the problem of somebody else at the Police Station. As he remembered, the Member hadn't wanted any charges brought then when the undergraduates had started behaving like the Class of '68.

Corbishley laughed. "A heckler? That's only the half of it, Inspector."

"Sir?"

"You should see some of the letters I've had recently."

"Anonymous?" asked Sloan. There had been some new laws lately about sending anonymous letters in the United Kingdom.

A smile twitched at the edges of the legislator's mouth: he must have known that too. "Not exactly anonymous, Inspector. They're all signed with a little drawing."

"The same drawing?"

The Member nodded. "From the Zodiac."

"A sign?"

"Oh, yes, Inspector. A sign and always the same sign. Sagittarius."

"The archer," said Crosby surprisingly.

"And I," said the Member drily, "am always addressed as Capricorn."

"The goat," supplied Crosby.

Perhaps, thought Sloan, the constable did read after all. His horoscope.

"But I," continued the Member easily, "have done very well in comparison with Ted Sheard."

"The Member for West Berebury?"

"None other. He told me, poor fellow, that he had a parcel of live scorpions in his post the other day." Peter Corbishley gave a light laugh. "So I didn't do too badly, did I, with just a heckler?"

BERTRAM MILLINGTON HERVÉ RAULY was still limping slightly.

"It was a very nasty sprain, Inspector. Caught m'foot in a hole in the carpet on the Saturday evening."

"Very unfortunate, sir." The carpets in Detective Inspector Sloan's modest semi-detached home in suburban Berebury did not have holes of a foot-catching size in them. Nor, of course, did he and his wife have as many carpets as the owner of Mellamby Place.

"The one in the Long Gallery," said Rauly.

There wasn't a Long Gallery in Sloan's house to have a carpet.

"My own fault entirely, Inspector," continued Rauly. "I'm always very careful about the one on the stairs. I forgot all about the other."

So there were two carpets with holes in them at Mellamby Place, then.

"Began," said Rauly, "to think that someone's hex was working."

"Hex?"

"Bone-pointing to be exact, Inspector. Found a chicken-bone under m'chair at the Garden Meeting in the afternoon." He frowned. "Don't like that sort of thing."

Sloan cleared his throat. "And the sprain was the evening before the battle, I think you said, sir." He made a note about the chicken-bone.

"I did," agreed Bertram Rauly. "And since," he added with a perfectly straight face, "if you go sick in the Army you're automatically deemed to be on a charge until the Medical Officer says you're really ill, I sent for the sawbones the next morning. Didn't want to be shot for cowardice in the face of the enemy or anything like that."

Sloan didn't for the life of him know whether the landed proprietor was being serious or not: the real Battle of Lewes had, after all, been a very long time ago.

"Dr. Lyulph said I'd probably sprained a ligament—and so I had," recounted Rauly, adding drily, "He's not an Army doctor, of course."

"No, sir." Sloan refrained from saying anything about police surgeons, who really did have to have their wits about them.

"Couldn't put m'foot to the ground anyway, so I knew I'd done something damaging. Managed to hotch myself about the place all right after a while but it was damn painful, I can tell you."

"Yes, sir, I'm sure——"

"And I definitely wasn't up to being William de Wilton that day."

"So . . ."

"So I telephoned Derrick Puiver. He was being the Battle Commander—we always have a Battle Commander in charge of Camulos Society battles, Inspector."

Then, thought Sloan privately, they were luckier than some in history who had had none. Or more than one.

"And told him about your leg?" he said aloud.

Bertram Rauly chuckled. "Better than that, Inspector, much better. I paraphrased the immortal words of the Marquis of Anglesey at Waterloo."

"Sir?"

"When he was hit by a cannon ball Anglesey said, "I have lost my leg, by God!" The Duke of Wellington was beside him and he said, 'By God, so you have!' "

"Really, sir?" It was funny how the Duke of Wellington had got himself so well remembered.

"What our Battle Commander said was, 'Blast, I'll have to find someone else.' And that, Inspector, is how poor Ottershaw got to play the part."

Sloan made a note but said nothing.

"He stood in for me while I hirpled about on the terrace getting in everybody's way." Rauly grunted. "Bad luck his dying on home leave like that."

"Very."

Sloan found himself being regarded by a pair of very bright china-blue eyes. "The Battle of Lewes couldn't have had anything to do with it, could it, Inspector?" asked Bertram Rauly shrewdly. "Seeing that you are here and all that . . ."

"We're just checking up on a number of matters generally, sir." Sloan was evasive.

"This and that," put in Detective Constable Crosby antiphonally.

"Ottershaw'd been out of the country a lot, of course," said the owner of Mellamby Place. "Doesn't do the heart a lot of good."

Through the centuries younger sons of the House of Rauly had come to grief in all manner of hostile climes.

"No, sir." Sloan turned over a page in his notebook. "If you could just tell me a little more about the—er—re-enactment, that would be a great help."

"It was one of our better efforts, Inspector," replied Bertram Rauly frankly. "The last battle the Camulos Society did before that was Waterloo and it turned out to be nearly as big a shambles as the real thing. So you will understand that this time the Committee was pretty determined to keep a tight hold on everything."

"Quite so, sir," said Sloan, wondering what Detective Constable Crosby was making of all this. "Tell me, sir, exactly what sort of fighting did you all go in for at the Battle of Lewes?"

Rauly waved a hand. "Mostly hand-to-hand stuff. Swords and so forth but for the actual killing——"

"Actual killing?" queried Sloan sharply.

"Within the context of the re-enactment," said Rauly, grinning. "We use a sort of crossbow with a special bolt of plastic material instead of an arrow."

"I should hope so, too," interposed Detective Constable Crosby in a sudden burst of rectitude.

The corner of Rauly's lip came down in a macabre twist. "Not as exciting as the real thing, of course, but I daresay you're both too young to remember that."

"This plastic bolt . . ." said Sloan touchily. The unspoken quotation, "Go hang yourself, Crito. We fought at Arques and you were not there," really struck home as far as Sloan was concerned.

"Inside it," said Rauly, "is some red dye. If that hits you, it's touché."

"Touché?" echoed the Constable, puzzled.

"It means you're dead," said Detective Inspector Sloan irritably. "And out of the game." Of all the games people played, he wasn't sure if this wasn't the silliest. He'd been finished with this sort of activity by the time he was twelve.

"Like Cowboys and Indians," said Crosby intelligently, "with knobs on."

"Exactly like Cowboys and Indians," agreed Bertram Rauly. "The extra ingredient as far as the Camulos Society is concerned is verisimilitude."

Sloan pushed his notebook into visual prominence. "I think it might be helpful if we knew who was—er—playing whom." The emphasis as far as he was concerned was on the word "playing." If he, Sloan, had a free Sunday morning in the summer time he spent it like most normal men did. Cutting the grass.

"Major Puiver, the Battle Commander, will be able to give you the full list, gentlemen, but as far as I remember Simon de Montfort was the Member of Parliament's Party Agent—a young fellow called Chadwick. David Chadwick. And the Curate was Gilbert de Clare. He was a bit of a wet."

It was quite impossible to tell whether Rauly meant the Curate or Gilbert de Clare.

"The King and Queen were Adrian Dungey—he's a vet in Rebble's practice, I always have him for the dogs—and Hazel Ottershaw." He screwed up his face. "I must say the outfit suited her very well. There's something distinctly flattering about a coif. Pity they went out of fashion. And then there was the Lord Edward."

"Who was he?"

"Henry III's son," said Rauly. "He was Edward I afterwards. You probably remember him as the Hammer of the Scots."

"And who played his part?" enquired Sloan.

"The Vicar's son—Michael Saunders. Then"—he grimaced—"there was Miss Mildred Finch, who wanted to be Fair Rosamund or Agnes Sorrel or someone equally unsuitable, but the period was wrong and I don't know what she did in the end. The costumes, I think."

Sloan made a note. A pellet might have made a hole in a costume. "Miss Finch?" he said.

"A retired schoolteacher of an interfering disposition," said Rauly. "Lives down by the church."

Sloan made another note.

Rauly said, "It was because of the Agent—David Chadwick—that we happened to have the Member with us on the Sunday as well as the Saturday."

"Don't tell me he got dressed up, too." Sloan had never seen Peter Corbishley other than properly clad for a public appearance.

Rauly shook his head. "Not he. No, he came out again because of Simon de Montfort."

"David Chadwick?" said Sloan, thoroughly confused.

"No, the real Simon de Montfort. He was the man who—so to speak—started Parliamentary government."

"Did he?" said Sloan.

"Got a lot to answer for, hasn't he, Inspector?" Rauly was grinning again.

"The Member, then," hazarded Sloan, "was there to make a speech?"

"At the end of the day," assented Rauly gravely. "He spoke about the Battle of Lewes and the Provisions at Oxford and the first recorded Parliament. Two burgesses from every shire or something like that."

"Bully for him," said Detective Constable Crosby. He'd been on duty once at a rural polling station on voting day and had been bored beyond belief.

"So," said Sloan, unsure whether Crosby had meant Simon de Montfort or Peter Corbishley, "you had your battle all right, sir."

"We did, indeed, Inspector," said Bertram Rauly, "but if anyone had been going to die afterwards I would have thought it would have been the Member rather than Alan Ottershaw."

Sloan lifted an enquiring eyebrow.

"There was someone who was present at the re-enactment dressed as the Figure of Death. You know the sort of thing, Inspector."

"I can't say that I do, sir."

"Someone covered from head to foot in black with a skeleton painted on the outside in white."

"Very realistic, sir, I'm sure."

"He seemed to me to be stalking Corbishley. David Chadwick, his Agent——"

"Simon de Montfort."

"—he noticed it, too, and got quite worried. Everywhere the Member went Death went too."

"There must be a moral there somewhere, sir," said Sloan lightly. If Crosby started to say anything about Mary and her little lamb he'd slay him then and there.

"That's just it, Inspector. Death turns up in a lot of early medieval literature. Take *Everyman* for instance."

"I daresay he gets all the best lines, as well, sir."

"What's that? Oh, yes, I'm sure he does." Bertram Rauly acknowledged this politely. "It wasn't that. No, the funny thing was that we didn't know who he was. Nobody knew."

"Nobody?"

"Not even the Battle Commander," said the owner of Mellamby Place. "Derrick Puiver hadn't got Death on his list of combatants at all. He didn't even know whose side he was on or how he came to be there in the first place. Odd, wasn't it?"

EIGHT

And a Man Is Uncertain of His Own Name

"DEATH!" thundered Police Superintendent Leeyes across his desk at Berebury Police Station. "What do you mean, Sloan, that someone was playing Death at Mellamby?"

"In costume, sir, at the re-enactment." The Detective Inspector had added the information to his report on his visit to Mellamby Place.

"Do you mean to stand there, Sloan," demanded Leeyes, "and tell me that the deceased had been playing Cowboys and Indians the day he was taken ill?"

"Soldiers, sir," said Sloan, clearing his throat. "Not Cowboys and Indians."

"Comes to the same thing," snapped the Superintendent. "Whatever they were playing at over at Mellamby they were old enough to know better. Death, indeed! Whatever next?"

Sloan himself knew better than to argue. "Yes, sir."

"With guns, you said," continued Leeyes with manifest disapprobation.

"After a fashion," agreed Sloan uneasily.

"What does that mean?"

"The Committee of the Camulos Society sanctioned two sorts of weapons for the Battle of Lewes."

"Stone the crows, Sloan," exploded Leeyes. "Who do they think they are? A bench of licensing magistrates?"

"Swords," persisted Sloan, "and crossbows."

"Oughtn't to be allowed," grumbled Leeyes. "Dangerous implements, that's what they are. Both of 'em."

"You don't need a licence for either," Sloan pointed out pertinently.

"Well you should," declared Leeyes, "and for everything else you can hit a policeman with—let alone a rabbit."

Detective Inspector Sloan, veteran himself of several confrontations with angry young men, said a silent "Amen" to that, and continued aloud: "I don't know yet, sir, if a crossbow was dangerous to Alan Ottershaw or not."

Leeyes grunted.

"It is known, sir, that he had a sword-fight with another—er—member of the cast called Dungey, Adrian Dungey. He's one of his father-in-law's junior partners."

Superintendent Leeyes snorted aloud.

"But," finished Sloan, "a queremitte pellet couldn't have come from a sword-fight."

Leeyes sniffed. "Are you trying to tell me, Sloan, and not very clearly I may say, that it could have got into the deceased from a crossbow?"

"I'm seeing the Battle Commander as soon as I can get hold of him," responded Sloan obliquely.

"Battle Commander?" Superintendent Leeyes' bushy eyebrows shot up. "It's worse than model railways, and they're bad enough."

"Enthusiasts," said Sloan. "That's all that they are, sir."

"So are quite a lot of law-breakers," retorted Leeyes swiftly. "You name it, Sloan, and we've got enthusiasts for it on our books—from speeding to little girls."

"Quite so, sir." Now he came to think of it, he, Sloan, was something of an enthusiast himself when he had the time. For growing roses.

"To say nothing of those who go in for art for art's sake."

"Sir?" Sloan's puzzlement was genuine.

"Forgers and fraud merchants."

"I gather," said Sloan, coming back to the point with the tenacity of a Robert the Bruce, "that the Battle Commander of the Camulos Society is a cross between an organiser and a referee."

Leeyes grunted. "And he's going to be persuaded to show you a crossbow, is he?" He leaned across his desk. "Tell me, Sloan, what do the Camulos Society use for ammunition when they're not shooting queremitte pellets at each other—if they were, of course?"

"Red dye," said Sloan, "contained in plastic balls which burst on impact."

"I see," said Leeyes. "Dye and you're dead." He seemed pleased with the witticism and added, "Do they get a lot of men who are dead but won't lie down or are they all on the Berebury Town Watch Committee?"

"I think the Camulos Society would regard that as cheating," said Sloan, into whose mind had floated a couple of lines of verse which had struck a chord in his schoolboy consciousness and had remained in his memory ever since:

> I'll lay me down and bleed awhile
> And then I'll rise and fight again.

He'd taken a lot of persuading by the English teacher that that wasn't a heroic couplet.

"What we used to say in our street when I was a lad was 'Bang, bang, you're dead,'" observed Superintendent Leeyes unexpectedly.

"Indeed, sir?" Sloan noted the remark for passing on to his friend, Inspector Harpe, the Traffic Inspector, the next time they met in the canteen. There was considerable speculation at Berebury Police Station about whether Superintendent Leeyes had ever been young.

"What about the widow, Sloan?" his superior officer was saying now.

"We've seen her, sir."

"I didn't mean to look at," said Leeyes impatiently. "I meant did she stand to gain or lose by her husband's dying?"

Sloan coughed. "I hadn't thought about that yet, sir. It's what you might call early days yet. All we've got so far is a hollow pellet."

"You should always think about that, Sloan. Always." The Superintendent had a Dickensian view of widows.

"Yes, sir."

"Well?"

"From what Constable Turton was telling us Hazel Ottershaw has never had to want anyway, being the vet's daughter."

"These big companies usually look after their own people quite well, too." Leeyes shrugged. "And nobody can say that the Anglo-Lassertan Mineral Company isn't big."

"After what the Member of Parliament said," added Sloan, "I'm arranging to see them as soon as I can."

"By the way, Sloan, while you're out and about there's something else you can do."

"Sir?" He hadn't even had time to look into the possible sugging in the shopping parade yet.

"It's the Member of Parliament for the West Division."

"Ted Sheard?" Detective Inspector Sloan turned over a new page in his notebook and waited.

Superintendent Leeyes picked up a message flimsy from his desk. "He's been having death threats through the post. Or so he says."

"Were they signed?" enquired Sloan.

"That's for you to find out," said the Superintendent, "but one thing is quite certain, Sloan, and that's that they've been posted here in Berebury."

TO SOME PEOPLE the twin professions of veterinary science and human medicine would seem to have everything in common, and at first glance this thought would pass muster. Indeed, disaffected patients of busy medical practitioners were wont to declare that their pets were treated by the vet with a care and consideration apparently well beyond the call of medical duty.

And worried farmers sometimes brooded on the fact that at least medical and surgical and hospital treatment for themselves and their families was free at what was the time of need for the patient and the point of sale for the veterinarian. Some of them were not above soliciting the opinion of the doctor on an ailing animal if he were at the farm visiting an ailing relative.

That both schools of thought were wrong would have been apparent had they happened to have overheard Dr. Brian Lyulph, general medical practitioner of Mellamby, talking to old Andrew Rebble, veterinary surgeon of the same parish, and father of Hazel Ottershaw.

The enquiries of the Criminal Investigation Department of the Calleshire Constabulary had not gone unnoticed by either man.

"If it wasn't a heart attack, Andrew," said Lyulph wearily, "then I'm damned if I know what it was."

Old Rebble nodded a grizzled head. Known himself over half the county as a good man with a labouring cow or an injured horse, he knew that Brian Lyulph was equally sound with ill humans. "Always start with the simple," he said.

That was part of the diagnostic process of both professions.

"And," he went on, "common diseases occur most commonly."

That was another.

"God knows," responded the doctor, tacitly acknowledging this, "Alan had everything you'd expect in the way of the signs of a heart attack, let alone symptoms."

It was a phraseology comprehended by the vet and he nodded again. His patients only had signs. Symptoms—that which the patient complained of—were a luxury denied to veterinary surgeons.

"He was sweating," said the doctor, "and he was having difficulty in breathing. In fact he was quite dyspnoeic."

Old Rebble jerked his head. "I know. I saw him myself."

"I'd forgotten that," admitted Lyulph. "He'd been sick, of course. There was vomitus all over his rig-out."

"There was marked pallor, too," said the vet, lapsing into the impersonal vernacular of both professions. They were both of them talking about a patient now, not a person.

"He was almost beyond speech by the time I got to him," said the doctor. "I'd been dusting off the Member of Parliament after that near miss with a lump of stone at the foot of the tower. He was all right, though."

"Alan wasn't." Rebble's expression was grim. He had a young widowed daughter and two grandchildren to think about now.

"No," acknowledged the doctor readily. "The poor fellow was obviously in great pain. I gave him a hypodermic injection of morphia *statim*—I didn't want to waste time trying to raise a vein at that stage."

"He was clutching his heart when I got there," said the victim's father-in-law, "so it hadn't worked by then."

"His pulse was all over the place, too," said Lyulph. "When I could find it," he went on, his voice pregnant with meaning.

Old Rebble nodded.

"And pretty rapid," said the doctor, obviously enumerating to himself a mental list of signs. Not for the first time, Rebble judged. "His blood pressure was way down," added Lyulph.

"It would be," said the veterinary surgeon. Animals had hearts, too.

And heart attacks.

"He had a cardiac arrhythmia, of course." Dr. Brian Lyulph was accounting to a well-informed relative. But only in a way.

"I thought he would."

"I found ventricular extrasystoles as well as an almighty tachycardia." He grimaced. "I thought he was going into ventricular fibrillation then and there."

"That happened in the Accident and Emergency Department at the hospital," said the vet sadly. "I went in with him and Hazel, too, remember? Though they sent us out into the corridor when he went into acute failure."

"The ambulance took its time," said Lyulph, unsure if there was an unspoken criticism in the air. "I was in half a mind to take it up with their Controller but I didn't in the end."

"It couldn't have been that the men didn't know the way," growled Rebble. "I recognised 'em. They were the same two fellows who came out the day before for that false call-out to the Member."

"I shouldn't think there's anything wrong with *his* heart," said Lyulph. "Cool as a cucumber."

"Nor with Bertram's," said the vet. "Do you know he walks right through the Chase every day? In season and out."

"Sportsmen like Rauly always get the right kind of exercise," said the general practitioner, who was too busy for either sport or exercise. "He doesn't overeat, either."

"You can't fatten thoroughbreds," said the vet absently.

"I can't honestly say, though, that Alan would still be alive today if the ambulance had got there any more quickly," said Brian Lyulph, coming back to what was worrying him.

Old Rebble was too experienced in the way of the world to ask him if he really meant what he had said. "Shouldn't have wanted a cabbage for a son-in-law," he said gruffly instead.

Lyulph grunted. "They shoot horses, don't they, but not men."

The ability to administer a *coup de grâce* legally was a powerful weapon in the armentarium of the veterinary surgeon but officially denied to the registered medical practitioner.

"And for all that the police want to talk to me." Lyulph shook his head worriedly. "I can't tell them anything more than I've told you, Andrew. I completed my part of the cremation certificate in all good faith."

"That's what Hazel wanted," said Hazel's father. "The young chap at the hospital said he could do the first part and she was very anxious that you did the other as you knew them both."

"The crematorium's medical referee wasn't unhappy," said Lyulph, "so I can't for the life of me understand why the police should be snooping around and wanting to see me."

"Neither can I." Old Rebble looked even older. "But, let's face it, they'll have their reasons."

"I'm very much afraid so."

The two men sat together in silence for a long moment, and then Andrew Rebble spoke. "Brian, we've known each other for a long time . . ."

Lyulph looked sharply across at the older man.

"I hope," continued Rebble, "that we understand each other, too."

Lyulph's expression changed subtly and began to assume its usual mask of professional inscrutableness. "So?"

"So, if there was anything—er—at all out of the way—untoward, say—about Alan's death, you'd tell me, wouldn't you?"

"There wasn't," said the doctor flatly. "Or, if there was, I didn't spot it." He got up to go, more worried now than when he had come. "By the way," he said, attempting to leave on a lighter note, "what did you prescribe for John Newby's sheepdog?"

The veterinary surgeon frowned. "It had a bad ear, didn't it? Oh, canker powder."

Lyulph grinned for the first time. "It's cured John's chronic middle-ear infection. Can you do anything for his hiatus hernia? I can't."

"NICE LITTLE CREATURE, isn't she?" said Adrian Dungey. "Don't let her put on too much weight, will you?" The young veterinary surgeon gave Miss Mildred Finch a quick professional smile as he patted her Bedlington terrier on the head. "You'll both live to regret it if you do."

"Certainly not," said Miss Finch, who didn't carry any spare weight herself, and whose dog Bebida was exercised and fed strictly according to the book.

"We see far too many chubby chops here for their own good." Adrian Dungey was the veterinary practice's small-animal specialist and, just as paediatricians develop dialogue skills with very little children, so he had come to extend his vocabulary of small talk with their owners. In the same way as his senior partner, old Rebble, had a good working rapport with the farmers of the district, so Dungey had a considerable following among the many single women with pets in the Mellamby area.

Miss Finch resumed possession of her dog but was clearly in no hurry to leave the consulting room. "Have the Committee decided on our next engagement yet, Adrian? I shall need as much time as possible if I've got to do the costumes again."

"Not that I've heard," said Dungey. His next patient was a Pekingese with bad breath and he was only too happy to let its owner wait a little longer. "Let's see, we've done all the interesting Civil Wars now, haven't we?"

"And the Wars of the Roses." They had been a great success.

"There's always the Battle of Hastings," said Dungey, "as long as I'm not King Harold. I never have liked," he added lightly, "that bit about ' 'Arold, with his eye full of arrow on his 'orse with his 'awk in his 'and.' "

Miss Finch toyed with Bebida's lead. "I've been wondering about Crécy myself."

"Good idea. The same armour might do."

She leaned forward. "But what would be really interesting, Adrian, would be an Old Testament battle."

"That's thinkable," said the young vet with the boyish enthusiasm which his clients found so attractive. "Gideon and the Midianites, do you think? Gideon was a really great general. I think you could almost call him the first of the management-selection people. Sorted out the good soldiers from the rest by the way they drank. Some cupped their hands and kept their eyes open for the enemy and some just plunged their heads down. Did you know that?"

"I," said Miss Finch, "was wondering about Saul and the smiting of the Amalekites."

"Coming down like a wolf on the fold, you mean?" He grinned. "That would be great."

"They spared Agag, of course," said Miss Finch enigmatically.

"He was the one who had to step warily, wasn't he?" said Dungey. "At least he did better than Harold."

"Coming down like a wolf on the fold would make a good charge," said the retired schoolmistress. "I've noticed that a good charge always goes down well with Society members."

"Old Testament weapons might be a problem," said Dungey, "even if the costumes were a doddle. I've never used a sling."

"Talking of costumes," said Miss Finch severely, "you got King Henry III's clothes into a pretty bad state at the Battle of Lewes."

"It was a great day," said Dungey, stretching himself to his full height. "Until poor Alan collapsed I enjoyed every minute of it."

"Not everyone did." She waved a hand. "Apart from poor Alan, I mean."

"Oh?"

"Didn't you hear?"

"What?"

"About the Member of Parliament."

"Peter Corbishley? Oh, old pinstripe isn't a Camulos Society member," said Dungey. "He only came back to Mellamby over the weekend to make a speech about Simon de Montfort and the first Parliament. David Chadwick said he'd persuaded him."

"I know, I know," said Miss Finch grimly. "On the Saturday he'd just got well and truly into his spiel when an ambulance turned up for him."

"I didn't know he'd been taken ill," said Adrian Dungey, surprised.

"He hadn't," said Mildred Finch. "That's the whole point. The ambulance people insisted that they'd had a message that he'd had a heart attack."

"And he hadn't?"

"Never felt better in his life was what he said to them. He told the ambulance men that he was as fit as a fiddle."

The vet frowned. "Odd, that."

"Mind you," said Miss Finch, "the ambulance crew didn't believe him at first. Apparently they quite often have turn-outs to people who don't realise how ill they are and who don't want to go to hospital."

"I've always thought that being a vet is easier," said Dungey, patting Miss Finch's terrier, "isn't it, Bebida? Not only can't your patients talk but they can't disobey you either."

"Or worry," said Miss Finch unexpectedly, "about themselves or anyone else."

"True. So what happened in the end?"

"Oh, the ambulance people went away after a bit and said they'd chalk it up as a hoax call. That wasn't so important but on the Sunday it was much worse."

Dungey leaned forward. "Tell me."

"Mr. Corbishley was standing at the bottom of the Motte tower when a lump of masonry came down and only just missed hitting him on the head. It was a near thing, I can tell you."

Dungey didn't seem very interested in the Member of Parliament. "The thing I thought was strange," he said, "was that odd black Figure of Death that was leaping about."

"Not as strange as I thought it," said Miss Finch astringently.

"I know it fits in with the period and all that but I can't remember his being on the muster roll."

"He wasn't," said Miss Finch.

Dungey looked up sharply.

"Moreover," said Miss Finch, "I wasn't responsible for his costume. I'd never even seen it before."

"So," concluded the vet, frowning, "we had Death in our midst without recognising him?"

"Just like in the old Mystery Plays," said Miss Finch, adding, "with a little Thornton Wilder thrown in." She was still cross with herself that she hadn't thought to bring the title *To Kill a Mocking-Bird* into her vote of thanks to the Member after his speech. "Staircase wit" Diderot had called that.

"I can see that there's a moral lurking about somewhere," admitted Adrian Dungey, "but I must say something in all this doesn't quite add up."

"Or," said Miss Finch profoundly, "it adds up to something very funny."

NINE

When the Last Sigh
Is Heaved

"ONE OF THE REASONS, Sloan," said Dr. Dabbe, "why the cremation procedure in this country is so comprehensive is that in the
nature of things the process destroys the forensic evidence. If such
there be." The pathologist stared down at the queremitte pellet lying
in an old Petri dish before him on his desk and amended this.
"Nearly all the evidence."

"But it doesn't affect the medical history, Doctor," responded
Sloan. "In fact I thought that cremation made writing down exactly
what the patient died from all the more important."

He and Detective Constable Crosby had gone back to the hospital
mortuary and were sitting in the pathologist's office.

"Naturally it does," said Dr. Dabbe. "I've studied the certification
in Ottershaw's case. It would appear at first sight," he said gravely,
"to be all in order."

"Ah."

"But, then," he added equally solemnly, "so did the death certificates of all those cases of cholera that the immortal Rudyard Kipling
described as being of the white arsenic variety."

Sloan pulled his notebook out: there was clearly more to Kipling
than met the eye. "You mean, Doctor——"

"That the certification is probably quite correct as far as it goes.
The cause of death was undoubtedly heart failure. I've had a good
look at the hospital case-notes and they record everything you would

expect to find in a patient expiring in that way—even unto the electrocardiogram readings."

"So the cremation certification procedure wouldn't present any problems to—er—anybody?"

"None. Ottershaw collapses at Mellamby. Brian Lyulph—he's the local general practitioner—examines him, diagnoses a heart attack, and gets him rushed to the hospital here. They pop him straight into the Coronary Care Unit and stick him on a monitor. He goes into left ventricular failure. They try to defibrillate but without success so it's——"

"Curtains?" said Detective Constable Crosby. He didn't like being in the pathologist's office—there were too many pickled specimens of pieces of human anatomy on the shelves there for his liking, but he preferred it to being in the mortuary.

"I couldn't have put it better myself," said the pathologist magnanimously.

Detective Inspector Sloan pointed to the queremitte pellet. "What about that?" Now he came to think about it "curtains" did seem the right expression for a death followed by cremation. There was something very like the end of a play as they swirled together after the coffin had trundled forward—the last exit.

"Ah, Sloan, what we haven't gone into is the cause of the heart failure."

"I see, Doctor." This wasn't Sloan's field and he knew it.

"The House Physician at the hospital had noted in writing all the things he had been told about the patient."

"Good boy," said Detective Constable Crosby.

"Just back from a desert country after a long air flight, took jet-lag badly, a sudden return to this country in what would appear to be conditions of acute anxiety—the House Physician said the wife was a bit hazy about the detail, but she knew about the stress—with the whole bang shoot being topped up with an energetic morning fighting a mock battle in costume."

"Pretty convincing," observed Sloan. "What you might call a cocktail of causes."

"Textbook," agreed Dabbe. "Even the blood chemistry tied in because they checked. And even if there had been a post-mortem I doubt if this little queremitte chap here would have come to light unless the cadaver had been X-rayed."

"And there wouldn't have been any call for that then, would there, Doctor?"

"Not if nobody had any reason to suspect it was there in the first instance."

Sloan frowned. "Is there any way of knowing how it—er—got into him? The cremation people aren't in any doubt that it did." This was an understatement. Those at the crematorium to whom Detective Inspector Sloan had spoken had been emphatic to the point of vehemence that there was no way that the ashes could have been other than those belonging to Alan John Ottershaw, could have been interfered with, muddled or otherwise confused in any way whatsoever.

"I can't tell you at this late stage, Sloan, precisely how it was introduced into the deceased's body, unless and until——"

"Yes?"

"—we know exactly what was in it. One might have a view after that."

"So it might have been swallowed?"

"Yes."

"Or fired into him?"

"Yes."

"What about the entry wound?" asked Sloan. "If there was one."

The pathologist tapped the papers on his desk. "According to these the deceased had had a friendly sword-fight that morning. You will be interested to learn that sundry small recent incisions were dutifully recorded as flesh wounds arising from—er—sporting activities. Nicely put, I thought that was."

"But——"

"And, Sloan, let me remind you that while actors tend to make bigger entrances than they do exits, with flesh wounds it's the other way round."

"Yes, Doctor."

"Remember the death of Nelson?" asked Dabbe.

Sloan started to say, "Kismet, Hardy . . ."

Crosby stirred. "Nelson? You mean that nasty little one-eyed creep who drank himself to death under the railway arches?"

"I meant Horatio of that ilk," said the pathologist grandly. "The musket ball that killed him at the Battle of Trafalgar left a hole only eighteen millimetres across and they've got his coat to prove it."

"Talking of proving——" began Sloan.

"With bloodstains?" asked Crosby with interest.

"Below the epaulette and left of the top button," said the pathologist.

"About Ottershaw," put in Sloan, valiantly trying to get back to the matter in hand. "We've established that they were using crossbows at this mock battle of theirs."

"Accommodating little weapons, Inspector," said the pathologist.

"I understand almost anyone can use them, too," said Sloan, "which doesn't help. Now, if it had been a long bow, that would have been different. It takes a strong man to use a long bow."

"A crossbow is what killed Richard the Lionheart, gentlemen," said Dabbe. "Did you know that?"

"No, Doctor," said Sloan. "About Alan Ottershaw——"

"Richard got it in the neck at Chalus," said the pathologist. "The bolt, I mean."

"From the blue?" asked Crosby.

"From the French," said Dr. Dabbe.

"About Alan Ottershaw," said Sloan for the third time. The pathologist was very nearly as rooted in the past as the members of the Camulos Society.

"He probably got it somewhere less sensitive than the neck," said the pathologist. "Somewhere like the front of the thigh—unless, of course, it was a case of 'I shot an arrow in the air, it fell to earth I know not where'."

"Yes, Doctor."

"Longfellow, Henry Wadsworth," said Dabbe. "A second-rate poet but a first-class translator."

"Quite so," said Sloan stolidly. "We've made an appointment to see the—er—Wardrobe Mistress."

"Then," said Dr. Dabbe, "the Forensic Science people will soon be able to tell you whether he was hit in his halidom or not. I can't. But"—the pathologist's mood and manner changed mercurially—"what they won't be able to tell you—and neither can I—is whether there was any substance contained in that pellet which could have brought about a heart attack."

"But they do exist?" Sloan seized on what looked like a fact. They were short on facts so far.

"Indeed, they do," said Dr. Dabbe. "Most native arrow-tip and blow-dart poisons come into this category and so do whole pharmacological families of drugs in quite common medicinal use. Starting with the foxglove."

"What about scorpion stings?" asked Sloan suddenly.

The pathologist frowned. "The venom causes intense pain. I do know that. But unless the pellet happened to hit the victim in the chest——"

"Was aimed at the heart," said Sloan mordantly.

"—was aimed at the heart," conceded Dr. Dabbe with unimpaired amiability, "he would have had so much pain at the entry site that he would have been bound to tell someone. That point would then have been examined at once and the entry wound found by the general practitioner on the spot."

"You've got to catch your scorpions, too, sir," contributed Crosby, "and that doesn't come easy in Calleshire."

"Quite apart from the fact that scorpions discharge an irritant poison designed to paralyse their enemies and prey," continued the doctor. "Not a stimulant designed to bring about heart failure." He turned to Crosby. "Catching scorpions isn't a problem, Constable. Not in Calleshire, anyway. They've got plenty in the Biology Laboratories at the University and I daresay that animal research institute at Pletchford could rustle you up a few if you're short."

"To say nothing," said Sloan, making a note, "of Toad Hall or whatever they call that reptile place over at Almstone."

AT VERY MUCH the same time as Adrian Dungey was steeling himself to examine a Pekingese with offensive breath in his surgery at Mellamby in the English county of Calleshire, Sheikh Ben Mirza Ibrahim Hajal Kisra was granting an audience to Mr. Anthony Mainwaring Heber Hibbs at his palace at Bakhalla to the north of the capital of Lasserta, Gatt-el-Abbas.

News of the death of Alan Ottershaw had reached the Sheikhdom of Lasserta rather more quickly than it had the Police Station in

Berebury, but Sheikh Ben Hajal Kisra had chosen not to respond to the intelligence until now.

Her Britannic Majesty's Ambassador agreed (in a manner highly redolent of "The Tale of Solomon Grundy") that Alan Ottershaw had been ill and was now dead and very nearly buried.

"I understand," said the Sheikh ambiguously, "that in the West these matters take time."

"Yes, indeed," said Heber Hibbs.

"In Lasserta," said the Sheikh, "everything is always done by sundown."

"Lassertan celerity in all matters is very commendable," observed the Ambassador cautiously.

This was not strictly true.

There was the little matter of the ancient rite still performed by the Lassertans known as the Massacre of the Kinsmen. This was the permitted swift and wholesale slaughter of the relatives of a new king uncertain of his throne. While it was an aspect of Lassertan speediness that did not go down very well in the West these days, the Ambassador was bound to admit that it did make for a certain political stability and a secure monarchy. Nobody could say that there was anything tentative about Ben Hajal Kisra.

"Expedition," said the Sheikh, baring his teeth in what in a lesser man might have passed for a smile, "is the hallmark of good government." Since queremitte ore had begun to be mined in Lasserta, the Sheikh had become considerably more knowledgeable about hallmarks.

"Would that there were more nations who thought so," responded the Ambassador with undiminished warmth. He had just realised that the Massacre of the Kinsmen was a practice that had, in fact, only died out in England with the Tudor Henrys, *père et fils*.

"Yours," said the Sheikh pointedly, "is a very slow government."

"The West is decadent in comparison with the East," said the Ambassador shamelessly.

Both men were only playing with words and knew it.

They had, in fact, a common end, but a necessary ritual had to be worked through before it could be achieved. All production at the queremitte mines at Wadeem had in the event been temporarily suspended by an anxious Anglo-Lassertan Mineral Company soon after

Alan Ottershaw had left the country and before the Sheikh's deadline had been reached. The Ambassador had been charged by a worried Foreign Office—spurred on by a concerned Ministry of Defence Procurement—with getting the mines working again. The Anglo-Lassertan Mineral Company's profile in this manoeuvre was too low to be visible at all.

Sheikh Ben Hajal Kisra, who could do mental arithmetic on royalties per tonne of ore mined as well as the next man provided the sums were large enough, was just as keen as the Ambassador to have production at Wadeem restored but could not say so without losing face.

In fact he said—or, rather, quoted—the exact opposite. "If necessary we can go back to the desert."

The Ambassador fixed his gaze on the baldaquin above the Sheikh's head and said, "I hear—this, Your Highness, is just market gossip, you understand—"

In another culture market gossip would be called "uninformed sources" and in yet another "newspaper speculation." This, however, was the Middle East.

"It is an old Lassertan proverb," responded Sheikh Ben Hajal Kisra, "that what is spoken in the souk today happened yesterday or tomorrow."

"I hear," repeated Anthony Heber Hibbs mendaciously, "that Your Highness's neighbour to the north is even now actively considering allowing a geological survey team into his benighted country."

Sheikh Ben Hajal Kisra, as always, stiffened at the mention of his northern neighbour. The Sultanate of Zonaras was seldom even named in Lasserta, and exploration shafts there looking for queremitte or anything else were certainly not to be encouraged.

"It would be a pity," remarked the Ambassador guilelessly, "if Lasserta—er—went back to the desert and Zonaras so to speak came in from it instead." He very nearly used a metaphor about coming in from the hot but thought better of it just in time.

His Highness Sheikh Ben Mirza Ibrahim Hajal Kisra said in a detached way, "The debt of death to Lasserta has been repaid."

The Ambassador nodded. Lassertans lived by the Mosaic law of an eye for an eye, a tooth for a tooth.

"A death for a death," said the Sheikh.

The Ambassador lowered his head in assent again, still keeping silent. The Foreign Office had told him that Alan Ottershaw's illness had appeared to have been genuine, but neither he nor Malcolm Forfar of the Anglo-Lassertan Mineral Company had seen fit to apprise the Lassertans of this.

"I have decreed," said the Sheikh, "that no servant of the Anglo-Lassertan Mineral Company shall drive a vehicle in Lasserta ever again."

The Ambassador bowed. Under Mosaic law that would be a speedometer head for a steering arm. Or something.

"In future," declared the Sheikh, "my people will do their driving for them."

"An excellent idea, Your Highness," said Anthony Heber Hibbs. "What could be better?"

"Then," said Ben Kisra, "nothing so unfortunate as the murder by motor car of a Lassertan by a European can occur in future."

"A very wise precaution," agreed the Ambassador blandly, totally suppressing the view expressed in cable after cable by a preternaturally suspicious Whitehall that for "accident" one should read "incident." "It would be preferable," he added carefully, "not to have production at risk a second time."

The Sheikh said nothing.

"A steady extraction of ore," went on Heber Hibbs, "would seem to be in the best interests of everyone, except, of course," he added, "the Sultan of Zonaras."

There was yet another pause while a knighthood for the Ambassador in the next Birthday Honours hung in the balance.

"So be it," said the Sheikh, clapping his hands in the Lassertan equivalent of the Royal Assent, adding gnomically, "Death is a camel that lies down at every door."

TEN

And the Last Tear Shed

DETECTIVE CONSTABLE CROSBY didn't really want to visit the premises of Morton and Son, Funeral Furnishers. "Couldn't Tod come round to us, sir?" he asked when he was told about it.

"No, Crosby, he couldn't." Detective Inspector Sloan was quite firm. "If he's got any records about the deceased then they'll be there, not at the Police Station."

"I don't see how he can tell us anything, anyway," objected the Constable.

"When the Superintendent says to leave no stone unturned, Crosby, he means it." This was unfair and Sloan knew it: his own inclination was to thoroughness too.

Crosby changed tack. "Tod might be out on a job when we get there."

"Then we'll wait," said Sloan.

"Wait there?" Crosby sounded even more unhappy.

"Why not? After all, Mortons do call it a funeral parlour." Detective Inspector Sloan collected up his notebook and started for the door. "And if Tod isn't there we can always sit down quietly and wish we'd led better lives."

In the event they didn't have to.

Tod Morton had just got back to his office after arranging a funeral when the two policemen arrived there. He continued taking off his black Edwardian-style frock-coat, and then hung it carefully on a coat-hanger.

"I can remember," remarked Sloan, "when that sort of rig-out used to spell trouble down at the Police Station."

"That wasn't yesterday," said Tod respectfully.

"Teddy-boys used to wear it—velvet collars and all." Sloan settled himself more comfortably into a chair that was clearly meant for the newly bereaved.

"It's all right still if you're a man," said Tod gloomily, "but there are ladies coming into the business more and more these days——"

"Nothing's sacred any more," said Crosby histrionically.

"—and they have the devil's own job not looking like the Wicked Fairy at the Christening. Everything except the broomstick."

They had Equal Opportunity down at the Police Station, too. That meant that the women got the rough end of "domestics."

"Doesn't do the trade any good at all, I can tell you," said Tod. "The only thing the ladies are good for is a laugh, that's what I say." He glanced quizzically at Sloan. "You're not here for a laugh, though, are you, Inspector?"

"No, Tod." Sloan looked round the subtly furnished waiting room. "Like everyone else who calls here, it's strictly business."

"I thought," said the young undertaker, "that it might be a case of 'don't ring us, we'll ring you.' "

"And we thought, Tod, that your memory might work better on your home ground."

"Fair enough." Tod insinuated himself into an ordinary jacket and looked years younger at once. "What do you want to know?"

"Everything you can remember about the Ottershaw funeral," said Sloan.

"Ah, Inspector, there *was* something then."

"A pellet," replied Sloan smoothly. "The one which you showed us."

"So you're not telling."

"It's always the coppers who ask the questions, Tod. You should know that."

"Like what sort of questions?"

"How did you get on with the widow?"

Tod relaxed. "The first thing you grasp in our line of business, Inspector, is that it doesn't do to call 'em widows. Not as soon as that. They don't know who you mean and to begin with they never think it's them."

"Learned that at your father's knee and other low joints, did you?" asked Crosby sardonically.

Tod looked pained. "The state of widowhood takes time to get used to, that's what I meant, and we just don't use the term first time round. Besides," he said readily enough, "it was the father-in-law who made all the arrangements. He told us his daughter was much too upset to do anything and we were to get in touch with him if there were any queries. Seemed a sensible sort of a fellow. Businesslike, anyway."

Sloan nodded. Undertaking was probably the only trade where you had to mix sentiment with business to do well.

"And not young. I should say he was getting on for sixty-five. I could turn his name up for you, if you like."

"It was Andrew Rebble," said Sloan. "He's the veterinary surgeon at Mellamby."

"He seemed to know the form," said Tod, "which is always a help."

Detective Constable Crosby stirred. "You have trouble with first-time buyers, then, do you, Tod?"

"You try explaining death certificates and burial orders to the nearest and dearest," retorted Tod a trifle heatedly, "straight after their first death in the family and you'll soon find out all about the little local difficulties." He drew breath and carried on in the same vein. "And that's without bringing in the sextons and the grave-diggers. On a bad day Cemetery Sid can complicate the simplest funeral. In my humble opinion children should be taught all about funerals at school. To my mind they teach 'em a deal too much about life and not half enough about death."

"All right, all right," said Crosby pacifically. "No need to get aerated. Sorry I asked."

"To say nothing about vicars," Tod went whingeing on. "Officiating clergymen aren't always sweetness and light by any manner of means. Oh, no, not when they're standing out on the clay among the dripping yew trees in the rain."

Detective Inspector Sloan tapped his notebook with his pencil.

"Were there, in fact, any problems with this funeral, Tod? About certificates and so on?"

"Not that I know of," said Tod, his ire subsiding as quickly as it had arisen. "Like I told you, Inspector, it was certified as heart failure. The client hadn't died of anything contagious or the hospital would have told us. There's a communicable diseases routine, you know."

Sloan nodded. An undertaker, of course, would be one of the people who would know the difference between infection and contagion.

"Can't be too careful, can you, Inspector, with all these new diseases about. Get rid of one like smallpox and up pops Aids. Seems there's always going to be a plague around of one sort or another."

"About the funeral, Tod," Sloan reminded him.

"Ah, yes, the funeral. Where was I?" He frowned. "I remember now. This Mr. Rebble comes along and makes all the arrangements, like I said. Only two cars wanted because they all live near the church and it's family only at the cremation."

"Those cars that you use—" began Crosby, finding something that did interest him at last.

"And then . . ." said Tod.

"Yes?" Sloan's pen was poised over his notebook.

"Then the deceased's employers came into the picture." He screwed up his brow in an effort of recollection. "The Anglo-Lassertan Mineral Company. I think they must charge their wreaths to their advertising budget."

"Very probably."

"Well, they hired the rest of the fleet to collect them at Berebury Station."

"And get them to the church on time?" suggested Crosby mordantly.

"You've got it in one," said Tod.

"Tell me about them," Sloan invited the undertaker. The Anglo-Lassertan Mineral Company was high on his list of those to be interviewed as soon as possible.

Tod Morton didn't need asking twice. "A funny lot, they were, Inspector. It was like they were in uniform. All dressed the same. Black, of course. Their leader was a short, thick-set chap."

"So was Napoleon," said Sloan. "Go on."

"The rest moved in a sort of . . . a sort of phalanx behind him. A bit like ducklings following a mother duck. Watched everything like a hawk, their great white chief did, and all the others watched him."

"What was there to watch?" asked Sloan.

"Not a lot." Tod scowled. "Not that I can remember, anyway."

"You collected the body from the hospital mortuary first," prompted Sloan.

"And brought it back to our Chapel of Rest." Tod brightened. "We've got a lovely Chapel of Rest, Inspector. Would you like to see it?"

"No," said Sloan. "Go on."

"On the day of the funeral our hearse takes the coffin over to Mellamby Church—"

Detective Constable Crosby chose this moment to chant with unseemly levity, "It wasn't the cough that carried him off, it was the coffin they carried him off in."

"Straight to the church?" enquired Detective Inspector Sloan, deciding to rise above this.

"That's right, Inspector," said Tod. "The widow didn't want the children to see it."

"And then?"

"The Vicar meets us at the undertaker's rest."

"The what?"

"The lych-gate." Tod grinned. "Didn't you know that was what they were?"

"No," said Sloan.

"Before clocks," said Tod Morton, "the family'd take the coffin as far as the lych-gate and just wait there until the parson came to take the funeral service."

"Would they, indeed?" said Sloan. "Well, we've got clocks, Tod, and they're ticking away."

"The Vicar leads the way from there on and we move into God's Acre. You know what that is, don't you?"

"Just keep going, Tod, that's all."

"And we get to the church."

"Dead on time," remarked Crosby unnecessarily.

"What about the service?" asked Sloan. He would deal with Crosby later.

"Ah," said Tod, "I'm afraid you'll have to ask someone else about that."

"You didn't stay?" Sloan was surprised.

"Have a heart, Inspector. How many times a day could you bear to listen to 'For All the Saints Who from Their Labours Rest' followed by 'Abide With Me'?"

Sloan agreed that it might get a man down in the long run.

"Better than 'Smoke Gets in Your Eyes,'" said Crosby irreverently.

"I buried a butcher and grazier once," said Tod, momentarily diverted, "and they sang 'Sheep May Safely Graze' at the service."

"They never!" said Crosby.

"Tod," began Sloan dangerously, "the Ottershaw funeral . . ."

"All right, all right." Tod jerked his head in the direction of sounds coming from his yard. "Like I said, I didn't stay myself and the boys——"

"The pall-bearers?"

"Them." Tod nodded. "Melvin and his mates—they went and sat out on a grave somewhere. They like the table-top ones best for sitting."

"Marble chips would be uncomfortable," said Crosby. "I can see that."

Sloan tapped his notebook. As he remembered it, table graves had been designed to frustrate nineteenth-century resurrectionists, not for providing seating for pall-bearers. "And had a smoke, I suppose?" he enquired.

"All except Garry," replied Tod.

"What did Garry get up to?" asked Sloan, resigned now to hearing everything—but everything—about Alan Ottershaw's funeral as patiently as he could.

"He's into churchyard flowers."

"Pinching them from the graves and selling them, you mean?" asked Crosby. Some of the offences which he had been taught about at the Police Training School were more heinous than others.

Tod looked pained. "Certainly not. Looking for wild flowers."

"Pansy, is he?" suggested Crosby.

It had not occurred to Detective Inspector Sloan that a conversation about flowers could get out of hand so easily. At the back of his own mind there was lurking something of Wordsworth's that he had been made to learn at school about churchyard flowers. In his view William Wordsworth was not a man's poet at all but the imagery of those verses had stuck through the years. It had conjured up a scene of grave mounds large and small. And a courteous parson—"the calm delights of unambitious piety, he chose, and learning's solid dignity." There had been the memory of a woman, too. Ellen, poor Ellen. That was it. Learning's solid dignity had been heavily stressed at Sloan's school. He said aloud, "What did you do then, Tod, while the service was going on?"

"Popped out of the west door because it's at the back, see?"

"And so nobody sees you skiving off," said Crosby, who knew more than a little about skiving himself.

"You've got it in one," acknowledged the undertaker, grinning. "First of all I went round and had a quick decko at where the ashes were to go."

"Under the east window, you told me," said Sloan.

"That's right. You'd be surprised how often it's under the east window, Inspector."

"Would I?" asked Sloan, who thought he would no longer be surprised at anything.

"That's a sort of harking back to the olden days."

"Is it?" said Sloan, mystified. Tod was too young to be automatically associating the olden days with the golden days.

"When they used not to allow the unconsecrated to be buried in churchyards."

"Felons, you mean?" contributed Crosby intelligently. "And Susansides?"

"That's right."

"What's that got to do with—" began Sloan.

"So," said Tod, "they used to bury them outside the churchyard but as near to the altar as they could get."

"Making the best of both worlds," responded Sloan before he'd quite thought the remark through.

"That's right," said the undertaker. "And those clients who aren't really and truly into cremation even though they have it done, they go for having the ashes chest interred in the churchyard under the east window."

"Then what did you do?" asked Sloan valiantly. "After you'd inspected the ground."

"Went back to the west door and kept an ear open for clues about when the service would be over. An organ is a great help at a funeral."

"I'm sure," said Sloan astringently.

"Mind you, Inspector, the Vicar took his time anyway, so I was all right. Sometimes you get a real speed merchant."

"A quicker vicar," suggested Detective Constable Crosby insouciantly, "or a faster pastor."

"And then you can be in trouble," finished Tod.

"Trouble?" rasped Sloan. "What sort of trouble?"

"Too early at the crem, of course," said Tod, surprised. "That's always bad."

"Yes, I can see that," agreed Sloan. Every man to his own trade.

"But if the family go in for people speaking verse and suchlike, then you know they've worked the timing out properly and that it will be all right." The undertaker warmed to his theme. "If I had a fiver for every time I've heard Tennyson's 'Crossing the Bar'——"

"The Ottershaw funeral, Tod," said Sloan again. As a working policeman he did not himself subscribe to the old Poet Laureate's sentiments about letting there be no moaning at the bar when he put out to sea. He, Christopher Dennis Sloan, was all in favour of decent mourning and had instructed his wife Margaret on the matter. Not *pompes funèbres* with black plumed horses but a proper send-off all the same. With roses. If in bloom.

He gave himself a metaphorical shake. This was what came of conducting interviews in an undertaker's parlour.

"The Ottershaw funeral," he said yet again. "What happened then, Tod?"

"Oh, they had an encomiast so it was all right."

"A what?" said Sloan.

"You know, Inspector." Tod grinned. "Someone who has the nerve to stand up and say what a grand chap the deceased was. Same as that bit about not speaking ill of the dead but with all the trimmings and a side salad."

"De mortuis nil nisi bonum," said Sloan. It was probably the only Latin tag that nearly all Murder Squad detectives knew—and that was because the feeling so often got in the way of an investigation. Especially a murder investigation.

"Could be," assented Tod cheerfully.

"Who spoke it?" asked Sloan. On police ceremonial occasions the Assistant Chief Constable of the County of Calleshire, who was an Old Boy of a famous school, was nearly always the one wheeled on. He had a favourite quotation from Juvenal which usually found its way into his public addresses. Except funerals, of course. Translated, it meant that no one ever reached the climax of vice at one step. He declaimed it to benches of magistrates as often as he could: judges didn't need telling.

"A guy from his firm," responded Tod. "The head one, I should say, from the way the others treated him. Behaved as if they were a bit afraid of the boss, they did," he added reflectively. As an employer Tod Morton was as soft as pussy's foot. "Why do you want to know about the funeral, Inspector?"

"If we'd known about the pellet, Tod, we'd have been there ourselves. Because we didn't, you will have to be our eyes and ears."

"What else do you want to know?"

Sloan wasn't sure how to put something almost intangible. "If we'd been there ourselves, Tod, we'd have—well, caught the flavour."

"I get you," said Tod promptly. "Well, there was a heavy local presence—you can always tell—and, as I told you, his colleagues were there in strength." He wrinkled his nose. "The village nobs were there, too—Mr. Rauly from Mellamby Place and Major Puiver and suchlike folk. I recognised them."

"Anything else?"

"Nothing that I noticed." He frowned. "I gathered the deceased was known and liked but not very well known, if you get my meaning. Someone said he'd been away a lot. Plenty of sympathy for the widow and family naturally."

"Naturally," said Sloan. Hard evidence in this case was restricted to a small pellet made of queremitte. "Can you tell me the name of the—er—encomiast?" It was high time they established a little more about the late Alan Ottershaw.

"Hang about," said Tod, "and I'll find out." He grinned. "I expect you've already spoken to the offilegium, haven't you?"

"The who?"

"Offilegium."

"And who's he?" growled Sloan. "If you're having me on, Tod Morton . . ."

"I'm not, Inspector. Honest. We buried the wife of the Professor of Classics up at the University not so long ago and he told me about them."

"About who, Tod?"

"These people. They were the people in ancient history who came to gather the bones after cremation. The washers was their other name and they anointed the cremated remains and placed them in the urn. It's a fact—he said so when I took him his wife's ashes, this professor."

"You go and find out about the encomiast, Tod," said Sloan: he supposed he had spoken to the offilegium at the crematorium. In a manner of speaking.

"All right," said Tod peaceably. "If you don't mind waiting for a minute." He grinned again. "I won't lock up or anything while I'm gone. Shop-lifting's not a problem with us."

"Gertcha," said Detective Constable Crosby.

"My girl'll have a note of what he was called somewhere." Tod left the room saying, "Bound to."

Crosby said into the silence, "Funny business, isn't it, sir?"

"What is?" asked Sloan sharply.

"Undertaking."

Sloan subsided. "It takes all sorts to make the world." In his own way, Tod Morton was as much an expert in thanatology as Dr. Dabbe.

The young undertaker was back in a moment. "Sorry to have kept you, gentlemen, but like we say in the trade, 'Better late than never.' "

Crosby groaned aloud.

"The head man's name was Morenci," said Tod. "Hamer Morenci."

ELEVEN

And the Coffin Is Waiting Beside the Bed

PRELIMINARY ENQUIRIES by the Calleshire Constabulary about the general availability in the United Kingdom of the hard metal queremitte had brought about a nasty attack of the shakes in the Head Office of the Anglo-Lassertan Mineral Company in London.

"Anyone would think it was a dangerous substance within the meaning of the Act," said Darren Greene, Vice-Chairman of the Board, waxing indignant at the police for asking about it. "The Health and Safety Executive aren't interested in queremitte at all."

"The Ministry of Defence Procurement are," snapped Hamer Morenci. "Very. And that's what counts." An executive suite panelled in afromosa wood and hung about with Modigliani paintings had been no guarantee of a full night's sleep for the Board's Chairman.

"I thought that Ottershaw's death would mean that we were out of the wood in Lasserta," ventured Darren Greene.

"Well, we're not, are we?" snarled Morenci. "Not if the police are sniffing around here asking us about queremitte."

"It doesn't look like it now," agreed the Vice-Chairman.

"It would seem, wouldn't it," said Morenci waspishly, "that it got us off the hook a damn sight too easily for the liking of the local constabulary?"

"His dying from a heart attack that particular Sunday struck me as so pat that I thought somebody's secret service had had a hand in it," said Darren Greene frankly, "but don't ask me whose."

Morenci looked straight ahead. "Every government's got its own dirty tricks department."

"Mind you," said Greene, "I wouldn't put it past the Ministry myself. They're dead keen on this new toy of theirs and as we know very well it can't work without queremitte."

Hamer Morenci said, "I don't think we can take anything for granted."

"That's just what the Detective Inspector said," Greene reminded him unhappily, "wasn't it? Before he asked us if we minded having our photographs taken."

Morenci put his elbows on his Charles Rennie Mackintosh desk and sank his chin between his cupped hands. Greene couldn't see if his eyes were shut or not, but he seemed to be replaying a scenario in his mind. "Listen, Darren, I only went down to Calleshire to make sure that everything was all right with Ottershaw."

"Sure, Hamer."

"I spoke with him on the telephone on the Saturday morning and he was so damned cagey I thought I'd better go down myself on the Sunday to see what he was up to."

"Good idea," said Greene pallidly.

"Well, what would you have done?" demanded Morenci.

"You didn't take the limo?"

"Hell, no! What do you take me for?" Hamer Morenci frowned. "No, I borrowed my wife's car. When I got there I found there were so many other cars in the village that Sunday morning that nobody can have noticed one more."

"How come?"

"A pageant," spat Morenci. "A medieval pageant."

"I thought maypoles had gone out when fertility drugs came in."

The Board Chairman was brooding too much on his own troubles to smile. "And to make it worse nearly everybody was wearing fancy dress."

"Even Ottershaw?"

"Even Ottershaw. Although I didn't know then," Morenci said. "I haven't got X-ray eyes, have I?"

"No," said Greene, although he—and most of the employees of Anglo-Lassertan—had often wondered.

"I never even saw him then," said Morenci. "Not to recognise him, anyway. For all I know he was King of the Castle."

"Not Ottershaw," said Greene confidently. They employed industrial psychologists to assist recruitment and selection at the Anglo-Lassertan Mineral Company and those with designs on being King of the Castle were not taken on.

"Not that anyone's likely to believe me."

"No," said Greene. "They're not, are they?"

"As far as I could see everyone was up at the Big House." Hamer Morenci had come a long, long way from the obscurest of origins and it showed when he least expected it to. "There was nobody in at Ottershaw's address."

"You didn't leave your fingerprints on the front-door knocker, I hope?" It wasn't often that Greene ever felt he had the upper hand in exchanges with his boss and he set out to make the most of it.

"I did not," said Morenci, suppressing any mention of having asked the way to April Cottage of a passing native of Mellamby.

"Then what did you do?"

"I went up to Mellamby Place with the crowd." This last was quite uncharacteristic. Hamer Morenci as a rule never went along with the crowd on principle. He frowned. "I saw Hazel Ottershaw but I kept my distance. She was being Queen Somebody or Other and enjoying it."

"What you don't know," pointed out Darren Greene, twisting the verbal knife to the full, "is whether Ottershaw saw you. You weren't in disguise, too, were you?"

"I wore my country tweeds," replied Morenci with dignity, "seeing as it was Sunday and I was in the country. My oldest ones."

"And you just watched, Hamer?" This was another tweak of the knife and they both knew it. It wasn't often that the Chairman of the Board played the role of silent spectator.

"Actually it was quite interesting," said Morenci defensively. "It turned out to be a mock battle. And not as mock as all that. Someone heaved a rock down on the crowd from the ruins of an old tower and while the fighting was going on round the castle other people were laying a feast out on great long trestle-tables on the lawn in front of the house. It looked big enough for a French wedding party and then some—although I must say the food looked a bit funny to me."

"Ottershaw," Greene reminded him. "You haven't said what happened to Ottershaw."

Morenci ran his tongue round his lips. "At exactly half-past twelve the fellow who seemed to be in charge of the battle blew a whistle and the fighting stopped."

"Just like that? I didn't think armistices were so easy to engineer."

"Those on their feet walked off and the dead and the wounded got up and they all set off towards this great feast." Morenci paused and ran his tongue over his lips. "Except one."

"Alan Ottershaw?"

"I didn't know it was him to begin with, naturally."

"Naturally."

"All I saw was a knight dressed in grey imitation armour with a red shield with a silvery-white chevron on it. A knight," said Morenci heavily, "who didn't get up when all the others did."

Darren Greene frowned. "So what happened?"

"When he didn't get up one of the others went back to see why. I saw him bend down over the chap lying on the ground, take one look at him, and then I heard him shout for help. They seem to have rustled up a doctor from somewhere and presently an ambulance turned up and the fellow was carted off. It wasn't until the next day that I realised that it must have been Ottershaw. I didn't know it at the time, I swear."

"Then what?" asked Greene, keeping the initiative.

"I came back up here to the office to see if there was anything fresh in from Wadeem. Forfar's hardly been off the telex since all the trouble blew up. That's how I came to hear that telephone message from Ottershaw on the tape."

Darren Greene nodded. Saturdays and Sundays were working days in Lasserta anyway.

"It was timed automatically," said Morenci, going over again ground already covered with the police. "Half-past nine that Sunday morning it must have been rung in. Before their tournament thing began."

"Are we quite sure it was Ottershaw?" asked Greene, although both men had listened to the recorded message time and time again.

"Oh, I know the voice said it was, but he's not exactly a familiar face at Head Office and the line wasn't all that clear, was it?"

"And it came from a public payphone, not a private line," pointed out Morenci. He smiled thinly. "Well, we'll soon know for certain if it was Ottershaw's voice, won't we, seeing that the police have got a recording too. They can check that with his wife."

"Widow," said Greene.

"Well, Ottershaw did say on the recording that he was willing to go back to Lasserta first thing on the Monday morning and that we could tell Malcolm Forfar so. And Sheikh Ben Hajal Kisra."

"Who's going to believe that?"

"No one," said Morenci. "Especially those two policemen—well, the senior one, anyway. I'm not so sure the younger one was listening."

"I certainly hadn't expected Ottershaw to ring up like that and say all of a sudden that he was willing to go back to Lasserta and face the music. Had you?"

Morenci's head sank even lower between his hands. "It was the last thing I expected. After all, he knows the Lassertans even better than we do." The Chairman's voice dropped to something only just above a whisper. "But I didn't kill him, Darren."

"No," said Greene dispassionately. "I don't suppose you did, but you must agree that it looks bad, doesn't it?"

MAJOR DERRICK PUIVER, unhappy while taking the chair at the Summer Garden Meeting of the Mellamby Branch of the Conservative Association, was unhappier still when talking to the police.

He had, however, it presently emerged, thoroughly enjoyed being the Commander at the re-enactment of the Battle of Lewes by the Camulos Society.

"The Sunday was much better than the Saturday, Inspector. Much. There was a heckler on the Saturday being very difficult at the meeting, to say nothing of having a false alarm for an ambulance and to cap everything else Mr. Rauly found a bone on the grass behind his chair. Most unpleasant."

"What sort of bone?" enquired Sloan steadily.

"He thought it was from a chicken's leg and I certainly hadn't noticed it before we all sat down. I must say I didn't like it myself.

I've served overseas, you know, so I know a bit about bone-pointing. Never expected anyone to go in for it in Calleshire."

"I can see that the Sunday might have been an improvement," said Sloan, making a note.

The Major puffed out his cheeks. "I think I can truthfully say, Inspector, on behalf of the Camulos Society that the day went well. Very well. Except, of course," he added hastily, "for poor Ottershaw."

He had met Detective Inspector Sloan and Detective Constable Crosby by arrangement at Mellamby Motte in the grounds of Mellamby Place. They were all standing together at the foot of the sole remaining tower of the old motte-and-bailey castle and were presently looking northwards. The Major pointed across the little dip in the land that contained the freshet that was the infant River Pletch and over towards the rise beyond and said, "If that had been Offham Hill at Lewes over there, Inspector, where the woodland begins—that's the old Mellamby Chase, by the way—then Prince Edward, the Lord Edward they called him, would have had his first view of the Baronial Army from this point here where we are standing."

"Quite so, sir," said Sloan, resisting the temptation to say anything about another possible theoretical and historical supposition: that if the wood were Birnam, then where they were standing was Dunsinane. "As it so happens, sir, we are—er—making enquiries about the re-enactment here at Mellamby rather than about the—er—original battle at Lewes."

"So I had heard," said Major Puiver. "Bad luck about poor Ottershaw," he added gruffly. "He was being William de Wilton, you know, and had to die early on. None of the King's party ended the day very well, of course."

Only Alan Ottershaw had actually died, Sloan reminded himself, but that had not been what the Major had meant.

"Except that the King fought like a Trojan," went on Puiver in his clipped military tones. "Lost his liberty but not his reputation, if you know what I mean. Difficult fellow to understand, King Henry III. Must have driven everyone to distraction." The old soldier's eyes took on a distant look. "Now, if it had been Henry V everything would have been different. He was a brilliant general and a real leader of men."

Detective Inspector Sloan put Agincourt out of his mind and looked across in the direction the Major had pointed. "So the enemy . . ." No, that couldn't be right: surely this had been civil war? He started again. "So the opposition attacked from over there by the wood?"

"That is correct, Inspector. For our purposes you may ignore the wood."

"Thank you, sir," said Sloan with deceptive mildness.

"Can't see it for the trees anyway," murmured Crosby under his breath.

"It was very important, though, to the original builders of Mellamby—the de Caquevilles—Inspector, because they held their land by right of cornage."

"Sir?"

"The de Caquevilles held their estate here by cornage," repeated the Major.

"That's what I thought you said, sir."

"That is, by the service of blowing the horn when required by the King," said the Major, "either to marshal his troops or to give warning of the approach of an enemy."

"I see, sir." Detective Inspector Sloan had had an uncle who had been a member of the Royal Observer Corps on the east coast during the last war. He supposed that was a lineal descendant of cornage in a way. It came to much the same thing, anyway. So did radar.

"It was also a means of measuring the ownership of land in times gone by," said the Major. "Instead of it being all yours as far as the eye could see, you owned all that where the horn could be heard."

"About the battle, sir." Sloan corrected himself as quickly as he could: "I mean the re-enactment."

The Major pointed towards Mellamby Chase again. "The Baronial Army took up its station over there on the rise and the King's party used this motte as their rallying ground. We didn't stick to the actual timing, of course, Inspector. Real battles tend to start very early in the morning, which doesn't suit amateurs. No, I didn't wave the starter's flag until half-past ten on the Sunday morning."

Sloan had read somewhere once about a tribe in Borneo—or had it been New Guinea?—whose warriors went to war in elaborate painted head-dresses of feathers and who were nevertheless afraid of the dark. In consequence all their wars had to be fought from nine o'clock to five o'clock, so to speak—in daylight, anyway—and on fine days because any rain spoiled their martial hair-dos.

"Moreover," continued the Major, oblivious of Sloan's train of thought, "since we usually fight on Sundays we always make a feature of luncheon."

Things, then, weren't so very different after all from New Guinea —or had it been Borneo?

"And then we normally have some sort of staged tournament or set competitive display in the afternoon for the children and the spectators and so forth."

"Fun and games," said Detective Constable Crosby.

"The real Simon de Montfort probably attacked just after half-past five in the morning, and that wouldn't have done for the Camulos Society members at all."

Detective Inspector Sloan solemnly agreed that verisimilitude could go only so far and no further. He said, "Perhaps, sir, you would just tell me exactly what happened to William de Wilton." He coughed. "Or should I say Alan Ottershaw?"

Major Puiver was impervious to irony. "As you know, Inspector, it was a role that Bertram Rauly had been going to play."

"Perhaps you could tell me who knew about the switch," suggested Sloan, trying hard to get down to brass tacks. "Apart from Ottershaw himself, that is."

"Me, of course," said the Major, "because I arranged it with him. The Wardrobe Mistress—that's Miss Mildred Finch—and probably the armourer. I don't think the Dapifer did because he wanted to know where Bertram Rauly was going to sit at the feast. Said someone had asked him."

"Dapifer?" asked Sloan tonelessly.

"A sort of steward. He was in charge of the eating and drinking. All the fare was medieval."

"Anyone else?"

"Ah, there you have me," admitted Puiver. "A lot of people knew about Bertram Rauly's injured ankle, and of course Hazel Ottershaw knew about Alan taking his role. She could have told any number of people." He cleared his throat in a hortatory way. "We call them roles rather than parts, Inspector, because we have a muster roll of the Camulos Society rather than a register of members. Or a cast list."

"And Mrs. Ottershaw, I suppose," said Sloan, silently gritting his teeth, "had brought her husband along that morning because he was there?"

"Like Everest," put in Detective Constable Crosby, suddenly waking up and taking an interest in the proceedings like the Dormouse at the Mad Hatter's Tea Party.

"Just so," said the Major. "Providential, you might say, I suppose."

If Alan Ottershaw had been inflicted with a fatal pellet that Sunday morning, thought Sloan, then it had indeed been Providential for him. In one sense, anyway. It had taken him straight to Kingdom Come.

Aloud, Sloan said again, "Who else knew about the change in par —roles?"

"I don't know myself how many people Hazel and Alan told," said Major Puiver. "I made a note on my muster roll naturally, and that might have been seen by other people. Must keep the paperwork straight otherwise you lose control."

Sloan hoped that Crosby was listening.

"I must say," carried on the Major, "the outfit fitted Ottershaw like a glove. Old Bertram's kept his figure very well. He's an old soldier, of course."

The little Major was still remarkably trim, too, noted Sloan to himself. He cleared his throat. "So, sir," he said, "as far as you are concerned unless the other—er—participants had been told by someone else or seen your muster roll they might well have thought that Alan Ottershaw was Bertram Rauly?"

"Indeed, yes," responded Puiver.

It was an unwonted complication as far as Detective Inspector Sloan was concerned. He changed his conversational tack, waving his arm towards Mellamby Chase. "This is all Mr. Rauly's land, I take it, sir?"

"It is indeed," responded the Major warmly. "And held by something a little more tangible than cornage, too, I'm happy to say. The Raulys did well under the Tudors but better still under the Stuarts.

That's when they built Mellamby Place. When James I was on the throne."

"The wisest fool in Christendom," said Sloan. Some historical quotations stuck in the mind longer than others.

"Not much of a campaigner, of course," said Puiver professionally, "but the Raulys themselves have always been soldiers. Right up to Bertram, that is."

"Don't tell me that his sons have gone in for pacifism," said Sloan. He'd had to restrain some very aggressive pacifists in his day and had scars to prove it.

"No, Inspector." Major Puiver shook his head sadly. "I'm afraid that's the whole trouble. The pity of it, I suppose I should say."

"Trouble?" queried Sloan, his professional instincts aroused by the word.

"He doesn't have any sons."

"Oh, I see . . ."

The Major said, "It's worse than that."

"No daughters?" offered Crosby brightly.

"No wife," said Major Puiver, adding sombrely, "And no heir, either."

"He might still marry." Sloan was bracing. "A man is only as old as he feels."

"Bertram had rather a bad time in tanks in the war," said the Major obliquely.

"What's that got to do with——"

"And sustained some—er—lasting wounds." He coughed. "It was most unfortunate."

"Stapped in his vitals, was he?" asked Crosby cheerfully.

"So," asked Sloan bluntly, "what happens to Mellamby Place when he goes?" In the First World War it had been the barbed wire that had taken on a legendary significance as far as future fatherhood was concerned.

"Ah," said the Major, "that's a very sore point."

"The National Trust?"

"He doesn't like institutions and anyway he can't afford to endow the estate."

"A really wealthy man could buy it," said Sloan.

"He can't abide the thought of strangers living here," said the Major, adding significantly, "and won't."

"Cats' home?" put in Crosby. He didn't like cats.

"So?" said Sloan, ignoring this.

"Bertram's told everyone that he's going to set the house on fire before he dies," said the Major.

TWELVE

And the Widow and Child Forsake the Dead

IT WAS A FULL HOUR after that before Major Derrick Puiver finished his conducted tour of the mock battlefield and what he called—several times—putting Sloan and Crosby in the picture. He came to a halt at last in the garden of Mellamby Place.

"We finished our day here, Inspector," he said, waving an arm, "in the old tiltyard with a little staged tournament and some troubadours. As it happens the real battle was over quite early in the day too. Simon de Montfort was a good strategist and the King's son—the Lord Edward, that is—although he was on the losing side at Lewes had learned a great deal about military tactics by the end of the conflict. Later on, of course, he did very well against the Scots and the Welsh."

Once again Sloan had a curious sensation that the little Major wasn't really sure which century he was in. He brought him firmly back to the twentieth with a question. "How easy, sir, would it have been for any participant to have fired a real pellet at William de Wilton. I mean"—hurriedly—"at Alan Ottershaw?"

The Major frowned. "You're postulating a sort of *der Freischütz*, are you?"

"Pardon, sir?"

"A free shooter, Inspector. A marksman."

"In a way," said Sloan cautiously.

"It wouldn't have been too difficult. Everyone taking part in the fighting was in their authentic heraldic colours." He coughed. "You may have heard that in the Camulos Society we pride ourselves on accuracy in all things."

"I had," agreed Sloan. They had standards in the police force, too, but he wasn't going to explain them now. Especially to a soldier.

"The whole idea of heraldry," said Puiver in a schoolmasterish way, "was that everyone should know who a knight was under his armour."

"So picking out William de Wilton wouldn't have been difficult?"

"I can't remember myself now exactly what his arms were—gules on a chevron three crosses crosslet fitchee of the field, I think—but Miss Finch will know. She's very sound on heraldic colours, too."

"But," persisted Sloan, anxious to get at least one thing in a very confused situation absolutely clear, "am I right in thinking that there would have been no way in which anyone who didn't already know about the changeover could tell that it was Alan Ottershaw inside that battledress and not Mr. Rauly?"

"You are, Inspector. Quite right. They were much the same height, you see. All anyone would have been able to tell was that there was someone there being William de Wilton." He gave a quick little cough. "Actually, as it happens, Inspector, we did have an—er —even more unknown quantity with us at the time."

"Sir?"

"Death." Major Puiver cleared his throat self-consciously. "I mean, of course, someone dressed as the Figure of Death."

"So we had heard." Sloan turned over a fresh page in his notebook. "And would you be able to tell me who that would have been, sir, might I ask? I daresay it's not everyone's part."

"You don't follow me, Inspector. By unknown quantity I meant that I didn't have anyone on my muster roll as playing Death."

"I see, sir," said Sloan impassively. "Death was an interloper, was he?"

"I certainly hadn't had anything to do with his being there," said the Major energetically, "although the Figure of Death crops up a good deal in a lot of early-medieval literature—*Piers Plowman* and so forth. Sometimes, of course, he's disguised as Winter."

"But you hadn't expected to see him that day at the re-enactment?" said Sloan with exemplary patience.

A moralist would have had a ready answer to that, but all the good Major said was, "Certainly not. I tried to question him myself but he only laughed at me and moved away."

Detective Constable Crosby stirred. "Wrong way round, that, isn't it?"

The Major swung round. "I beg your pardon, Officer?"

"I thought soldiers were meant to laugh at Death, weren't they?" said Crosby. "Not Death at them."

The detective instinct in Sloan asserted itself before Crosby got an answer to that. "I take it, Major, that Death didn't speak in case you recognised his voice?"

"Hadn't thought of that," admitted Puiver. "I just thought the fellow was being impertinent."

"Was it a male laugh?" asked Sloan curiously. Thanks to his mother, St. Francis of Assisi's Sister Death had figured prominently in his bedtime stories as a child.

"Yes," responded Puiver instantly. "No doubt about that but it's funny you should say something about my recognising him, Inspector."

"Sir?" Sloan searched about in his own memory: surely it had been in Chaucer's *Canterbury Tales* that Death had stalked about in disguise.

The Major frowned. "I did have a feeling that I'd seen him before but I couldn't for the life of me remember where or when. I couldn't place him but I felt all along that I ought to have been able to, if you know what I mean. I told our debriefing committee so."

"And whose side was Death on?" enquired Crosby with genuine interest.

He got a totally unexpected answer from Major Puiver, who said grimly, "Not poor old Peter Corbishley's anyway."

"The Member?" said Sloan alertly.

"None other," said the old soldier. "Death kept on leaping up and down in front of him wherever he went and doing a sort of war-dance." Puiver looked quite worried, and added seriously, "When he wasn't doing that he was stalking the Member round the tiltyard. And that was all before the Member had a narrow escape at the foot of the tower."

"Tell me," said Sloan.

"A stone fell from the parapet. Missed him by a whisker."

"THE TIME HAS COME, Crosby——" Detective Inspector Sloan stopped and immediately corrected himself. "No, the time is long overdue, Crosby, for a visit to Miss Mildred Finch."

"Yes, sir."

He led the way back to their police car, glancing at a piece of paper. "She lives at Capgrave Cottage, Church Street, Mellamby. Come along."

"Does that mean we're late, sir?" asked Crosby, taking this literally, and hoping to seize on a good reason for a nice turn of speed at the wheel. Driving fast cars fast was his principal joy in life.

"It does not." Sloan laid a wallet of papers on the back seat of the police car. "Nor does it mean, Crosby, that the rate of the journey calls for white knuckles on the part of the driver."

"No, sir."

"Or the passenger."

"No, sir."

"Just pretend your name is Tod Morton, that's all."

"Sir?"

"Drive me to Capgrave Cottage as if you were an undertaker behind the wheel of a hearse."

Even so it was not long before Crosby was asking where in Church Street, Mellamby, to look for Miss Finch's cottage. "There's the church, sir, but I can't see any names on the gates."

"Seeing that we call ourselves detectives, Crosby," said Sloan, peering out of the car window, "we might just be able to tell which one is occupied by—what did that chap Rauly call her? A retired schoolteacher of an interfering disposition."

"Yes, sir," said Crosby, adding insouciantly a moment later, "How?"

"From the front garden," said the rose-grower. "Gives a lot away, does a front garden."

"Yes, sir." Crosby slowed the police car down in front of a garden that was a model of neatness.

"No," said Sloan at once. "Not serried ranks of lobelia and salvia with alyssum in between. Patriotic, of course, and a very popular layout in the last war, but not sufficiently imaginative, I think, for Miss Finch.

The constable re-engaged first gear and drove the car forward.

"Nor the London Pride and day lilies next door, either," pronounced Sloan. "Ground cover, that's all they are. Lazy beds."

"Why they don't have numbers on their houses beats me," said Crosby, driving past a dwelling whose front garden appeared to comprise only an out-of-hand buddleia without even slowing down.

"A butterfly fancier," diagnosed Sloan. "Drive on—ah, try the one with the delphiniums and the lupins over there," commanded Sloan, his eye caught by a blaze of colour that would have done credit to Gertrude Jekyll. "Oh, and there's a really good eremurus in the border with some Blue Butterfly scabious—this looks a lot more promising, Crosby. Let's ask at this one."

A noisily defensive stance taken by a Bedlington terrier at the garden gate delayed the two policemen but brought a tall, gaunt-faced woman to the front door. As they advanced the policemen could see the words "Capgrave Cottage" carved on an oak board beside the door.

Sloan introduced himself.

"Police?" she said. "Ah, Constable Turton has been in touch with you then, has he? I hoped he might."

"Well . . ." prevaricated Sloan.

"It's disgraceful," said Miss Finch. "I don't know what this generation is coming to, I really don't."

"No, Miss." Sloan coughed and asked cautiously, "What have they been up to now?"

"Didn't Colin Turton tell you? It's the churchyard over there."

The two policemen pivoted on their heels and obediently looked in the direction of the churchyard. As far as Sloan could tell at a quick glance all the rude forefathers of the village of Mellamby were sleeping peacefully in their appointed places. "Something wrong, is there, Miss?"

Miss Finch sniffed. "Not now but there was until I put it right."

"Ah." Some citizens were better than others at the watch-keeping role.

She pointed. "You see that notice on the churchyard wall?"

"Yes, Miss."

"And what it says?"

"No dogs," said Sloan, feeling himself back in the classroom in an instant.

"It does now."

"So?" If the police were at Mellamby for anything, it was to try to establish whether or not a serious crime had been committed: not to examine notices on walls.

"Last night," said Miss Finch censoriously, "it was changed."

"Really, Miss."

"Last night," she paused impressively, "it read 'Do snog.' "

Detective Inspector Sloan's mind sought swiftly through a range of possible responses with the speed of a computer and settled for "That won't do at all, Miss. Can't have that on the churchyard wall, can we?"

"Certainly not," said Miss Finch.

"As it so happens, Miss, we hadn't come about—er—that." Sloan wasn't sure off the cuff what degree of misdemeanour could be committed by perpetrating an anagram. Would the legal eagles down at the Police Station construe "Do snog" as an incitement to violence? Or as coming within that archaic catch-all a breach of the peace? He said, "Actually, Miss Finch, we've come about William de Wilton." Which sounded just as arcane.

"Have you?" Miss Finch looked the two policemen up and down. "You'd better come indoors then. Come along, Bebida."

The Bedlington terrier gave a joyous yelp and made straight for Detective Constable Crosby's ankles.

"Bebida! Come here at once." Miss Finch smiled perfunctorily at the constable. "It's the trousers, you know."

"Quite so, Miss," said Sloan before Crosby could speak.

"I'm sorry," said Miss Finch, "but she just doesn't like men."

Like mistress, like maid, was what Sloan's grandmother would have said to that, but Sloan himself, wise in his own generation, kept silent.

A faint smile played along Miss Finch's thin lips. "She goes for Bertram Rauly practically every time she sees him."

"Indeed, Miss?" Sloan and Crosby followed Miss Finch inside the cottage and into a small sitting room to the left of the front door. "Doesn't she like Mr. Rauly, then?"

"She does not." Mildred Finch waved the two men into chintz-covered chairs. "No sense of history, that's his trouble, Camulos Society or not."

"You would have thought," murmured Sloan, "that living in a house like Mellamby Place . . ."

"That's the whole trouble," said Miss Finch warmly. "You would have thought so, wouldn't you, but Mr. Bertram Millington Hervé Rauly sees the most beautiful house in Calleshire as nothing but a millstone round his neck. Not as living history, which it is, isn't it?"

"Yes, Miss." On the shelf beside Miss Finch's fireplace Sloan could see a fine example of barbola work. That was living history, too, but at a different level.

"How he can bear even to talk of burning it down," spluttered Miss Finch, "totally defeats me."

"Quite so, Miss." Over Miss Finch's shoulder Sloan could see a wooden board with a motto and border design tastefully etched out in poker-work. Perhaps it was Miss Finch who had fire on the brain. "He's set on fire-raising, is he?"

If Bertram Rauly did set fire to Mellamby Place, that would certainly give the barrack-room lawyers in the Police Station charge room further food for thought. After all it was presumably his own property, but as it would undoubtedly also be a listed building within the meaning of the Act perhaps they would get him for wilfully damaging an ancient monument or something. Although if Bertram Rauly were dead or dying at the time that wouldn't do the Law a lot of good.

"So he says." Miss Finch pursed her lips. "He declares that he's going to burn the whole house down before he dies." She gulped. "And everything in it."

"I see," said Sloan. Happy the man, someone had said once, who didn't have any hostages to fortune in the way of a family. And yet without them fortune in its other sense didn't seem to have much meaning in the long run.

Miss Finch's voice trembled with emotion as she said, "And he keeps on saying he's getting old."

"He did fall, didn't he?" said Crosby pointedly, diverted by neither barbola work nor pyrogravure motto.

"Caught his foot in a hole in a carpet," said Miss Finch. "Or so he says." She paused impressively. "But I don't suppose he told you that it was a Savonnerie carpet."

"No, Miss," said Sloan. "He didn't." Oscar Wilde's Lady Bracknell would have said that the make of the carpet was immaterial: Miss Finch evidently didn't think so.

"He's got three Savonnerie carpets," said Miss Finch, whose own sitting room was covered in a good Axminster. She very nearly wrung her hands in anguish. "And he says he's going to burn the contents of the house with it rather than have any dealers pawing over his things."

"Does he, Miss?" replied Sloan thoughtfully. An unknown number of those present at Mellamby Place at the ill-fated re-enactment of the Battle of Lewes had had grounds for believing that Bertram Rauly had been playing William de Wilton. And the man who had actually been playing William de Wilton that day had died—with the medieval equivalent of an arrow in him.

"And the pictures," moaned Miss Finch. "All those beautiful pictures."

"Got some good ones, has he?" asked Crosby chattily.

Miss Finch looked at him. "Only one of the finest collections of Calleshire topographical drawings in existence."

Detective Constable Crosby looked quite unimpressed. "Can't understand myself, Miss, why anyone gets all excited about a painting of something they can still go and look at."

Miss Finch drew breath: she was a living exemplification, Sloan decided, of the old saying that you can take the schoolteacher out of the classroom but you can't take the classroom out of the teacher.

"If they want to," added Crosby, although Miss Finch had obviously already decided that he had no soul.

"To say nothing," continued Miss Finch, ducking the issue the Constable had raised, "of a series of oil paintings by Lady Butler." Throughout a long career in the teaching profession Miss Finch had never liked taking on hopeless educational cases.

"Lady Butler?" Sloan re-entered the conversation. He'd never heard of her.

"The doyenne of British battle artists." Miss Finch took pleasure in informing him. "A Victorian painter of great imagination."

"Seeing as she wasn't there at the battles," said Crosby egregiously, "she would have had to have been, wouldn't she?"

"I expect," said Miss Finch with totally misplaced optimism, "that *The Retreat from Moscow* is the one you probably remember best."

Crosby shook his head. "No."

The only battle painting that was firmly fixed in Detective Inspector's Sloan's mind was of chubby little Italians having a go at each other in the Middle Ages. The Florentines knocking hell out of the Sienese at the Battle of San Romano and an artist called Uccello making his own way into the school history books with something he knocked up about it a couple of hundred years after the event.

"Mr. Rauly has also got a representative collection of paintings by George Cattermole," Miss Finch went on with her lecture. Sloan hoped that her schoolmistressish tendency to impart knowledge extended to the matter about which they had come to Capgrave Cottage.

"Who's he?" asked Crosby simply.

"A well-known early-nineteenth-century watercolour artist who specialised in dramatic and romantic depictions of battle scenes. Mr. Rauly collects him."

"Does he, Miss?" Detective Inspector Sloan projected as much interest as he could summon up. They already knew that Bertram Rauly was a battle buff without Miss Finch's stress on the pictures at Mellamby Place. What was really intriguing Sloan at this moment was the question of exactly how the same patterned chintz that covered Miss Finch's chairs came to cling so tightly to her biscuit barrel as well. "Actually, it's about the Battle of Lewes that we've come."

"Poor Alan," said Miss Finch immediately.

"You knew him, of course, Miss . . ."

"Not well but as Hazel's husband." She gave Sloan a wry smile. "I used to tell her that she should put caraway seeds under his plate."

"Miss?"

"It's an old country recipe for keeping husbands at home."

"I'll remember that," promised Sloan. There was quite a lot of call down at the Police Station for something that kept husbands at home. Besides food.

"It works for hens that stray, Inspector."

"Mr. Ottershaw strayed then, did he, Miss?" It didn't, of course, follow that what worked down on the farm was effective round at the Police Station, Domestic Department.

"No, no, Inspector. Certainly not. That's not what I meant at all. It was only that in the nature of his work Alan Ottershaw was away a good deal and that's never a good thing for a wife and small family."

"Quite so, Miss." He'd heard that advanced as an argument against a prison sentence too.

"It was a great shock to everyone his coming back so unexpectedly and dying just like that." She shook her head. "A sad day for us all."

"Yes, Miss." Sloan coughed. "Actually, Miss, what we want to know is exactly what he was wearing when he was taken ill."

Mildred Finch looked at the policemen very sharply but said only, "His costume. It was rather heavy and it was a very hot day."

"Yes, Miss," responded Sloan easily. "That's one of the reasons why we thought we would have a look at it. And his armour and so forth." He didn't know if amateur armies had property baskets.

"It's in my spare bedroom," said Miss Finch. "I mend it through the winter."

"The Camulos Society doesn't fight in the cold, then, Miss?" said Sloan, following her up a narrow stair. Their likeness to the armies of New Guinea—or had it been Borneo?—grew at every turn.

"No, Inspector, it doesn't—do mind your heads on that beam, won't you—oh, I'm sorry, Constable, I should have warned you earlier, I've got a notice somewhere which says 'Duck or grouse' but I can't remember where it is—no, in the winter we revive the old custom of holding a Frost Fair." She led the way into a room full of costumes. "Everything's here."

It looked like it. There were garments everywhere and hanging behind the door was an old Leghorn hat, its fine floppy soft straw drooping now. Sloan couldn't decide if it was an artifact of mock battle or Miss Finch's own: Mademoiselle from Armentières could have worn it. So could Mata Hari.

"A Frost Fair?" he said aloud.

"That's right. If it seems as if there's going to be ice, Mr. Rauly dams the stream. If not, then we have it on the terrace."

The clothes in Miss Finch's spare room looked a total jumble to Sloan, but she paused only a moment before plunging her hand into a pile on the bed and coming up with a loosely woven grey string jerkin. "Here we are, Inspector. Imitation chain mail with gules on a chevron argent three crosses crosslet fitchee of the field."

"As worn by Alan Ottershaw?" asked the policeman.

"As worn by William de Wilton," said the Wardrobe Mistress of the Camulos Society.

THIRTEEN

The Angel of the Lord Shall Lift His Head

"THE WHOLE AFFAIR," pronounced Superintendent Leeyes grumpily, "sounds to me, Sloan, to have been about as dangerous as a masked ball."

Like Sheikh Ben Hajal Kisra, the senior policeman at Berebury took an essentially heliotropic view of the world. Nor was there any doubt in anybody else's mind—and certainly not in his—about who was the centre of the universe in "F" Division in the County of Calleshire Police Force.

It certainly wasn't a luckless Detective Inspector Sloan reporting on the police visit to the site of the re-enactment and the interviews with the Battle Commander and Wardrobe Mistress of the Camulos Society. There was no doubt about that.

The Superintendent sniffed. "All this dressing-up so that nobody's to know who's who."

"That's one of our problems," admitted Sloan. He took a deep breath. "Especially Death."

"What's that, Sloan? What did you say?"

"Nobody seems to have known who the Figure of Death was, sir."

"What did he look like?" asked Leeyes. "Tell me that."

"I gather, sir, it was a purely representational figure," responded Sloan. He himself had looked on death—and at it, too, which was something quite different—often enough to know the difference between fact and fiction. "It was played by a man covered from head to foot in black with the outlines of a skeleton painted in white on the material."

"Very realistic, I daresay," grunted Leeyes. "And did Death get all the best lines, eh, Sloan? Is that what they're complaining about?"

"No, sir. The trouble is that Death was unaccounted for by the members of the Camulos Society and nobody knew who he was."

"An outsider?" suggested Leeyes as unselfconsciously as Geoffrey Chaucer himself.

"Perhaps," assented Sloan. "Anyway, it's what makes his appearance important, especially in view of what happened to Alan Ottershaw."

Superintendent Leeyes, who never used a syllable when a grunt would do, grunted.

"Major Puiver," added Sloan, "said it was the sort of character that used to crop up a lot in the old Mystery Plays."

Leeyes was patently unimpressed. "It's the new mystery we're interested in, Sloan."

"Yes, sir. Of course, sir. That's why I'd like to see if anyone in Mellamby recognises a character called Hamer Morenci as having been in the village that day."

"In case he's your outsider?" divined Leeyes.

"Ottershaw changed his mind about going back to Lasserta," said Sloan, "after talking to the Member of Parliament on the Saturday afternoon and before he telephoned his firm to say so on the Sunday morning. The Anglo-Lassertan Mineral Company has given me a copy of their tape-recording of the message."

"What they say is a copy," said Leeyes automatically.

"I propose to check that it's her husband's voice with the widow, sir." The task might be in the line of duty but "nice work if you can get out of it" was how Sloan would describe that.

"Anything that might make sense of all this larking about in fancy dress," grumbled Leeyes, "would be a help."

"Yes, sir." In the comic papers burglars always wore striped jerseys and carried bags marked "swag": Sloan couldn't remember why. Not at this moment. But it did make for a certain simplicity.

"Whether it's suits of armour or mock shrouds," said the Superintendent.

"They're not quite suits of armour," explained Sloan. The convicts of yesteryear had derived the broad arrowheads on their prison suits from the livery of the family of Viscount Lisle and Dudley: he did know that. "No, sir, what they were wearing was mostly a sort of imitation chain-mail knitted with grey string."

"It sounds to me," said Leeyes trenchantly, "more like dirty dish-cloth than armour."

"The helmets are stouter. They do cover the head and shoulders for safety's sake."

"Safety!" said the Superintendent. "Pah! Much good a stout helmet did the deceased."

"Yes, sir." Sloan seized his moment. "We've sent the—er—garments the deceased wore that day off to the scientific people but even with the naked eye you could see that they were torn in all sorts of places." He hesitated and then went on more tentatively, "I'm afraid, sir, there's another problem about identification."

"Unless," insisted Leeyes, overriding this last, "you can see the whites of a man's eyes, I don't know how you can know who he is." The Superintendent had been asked to leave an Adult Education Evening Class on Social Anthropology for this and similar heresies. "No point shooting until then anyway."

"It's an extra complication, sir," began Sloan uncertainly, going on to explain to Superintendent Leeyes about Alan Ottershaw standing in for Bertram Rauly at the last minute at the re-enactment. "So," he concluded, "if anyone had intended harm to—er—William de Wilton, we don't know if the victim was to have been Rauly rather than Ottershaw."

Leeyes rolled his eyes heavenwards and demanded of his Creator what he had done to deserve this carry-on in his bailiwick.

Sloan hurried on. "As well as tracing the garments worn that day by the deceased in the hope that there might be a tear or a hole that would tell us something"—Sloan saw no point in mentioning banners with strange devices at this juncture—"we've looked at some weapons, sir."

"Well?"

"I have examined the crossbows used by the Society and fear that a real pellet——"

"Made of queremitte," grated Leeyes.

"—made of queremitte," Sloan tacitly agreed to the one fact that so far seemed to be beyond dispute, "could have been fixed to the bolt as easily as one of the Camulos Society's plastic balls of red dye."

"And do you have a second string to your bow, Sloan," enquired Leeyes frostily, "or are you sure it was aimed at Ottershaw?"

"I couldn't say, sir. Not at this stage." He hesitated and then added unwillingly, "There is even some doubt about whether Ottershaw—that is, William de Wilton—was the intended victim."

"And what, Sloan, might I ask, do you call that? Broadening the scope of your investigations? Or drawing a bow at a venture?"

Sloan stifled a number of possible replies to this and said in a controlled voice, "I understand the Member of Parliament narrowly escaped injury."

"Unless you make yourself clear, Sloan," snarled Leeyes, "you may not be so lucky."

"Yes, sir. I understand that Mr. Corbishley was watching the re-enactment from the foot of Mellamby Motte when a block of stone crashed down alongside him."

"And did it fall or was it pushed?"

"We don't know, sir. Not yet." Sloan frowned. "What we do know is that someone seems to have got it in for both Berebury's Members of Parliament. I'm told that the Figure of Death pursued Peter Corbishley all day at Mellamby."

Superintendent Leeyes muttered something quite indistinguishable about Guy Fawkes.

"And I hear," continued Sloan, "that Ted Sheard had a parcel of live scorpions through the post."

"Following up the death threats, I suppose," responded Leeyes absently, "though as to where you get hold of live scorpions in East Calleshire, Sloan, I wouldn't know."

"No problem, sir. There are several possible sources, and we'll be following them all up as soon as I've seen Mr. Sheard."

"I hear the death threats upset his secretary no end," remarked Leeyes. "Sheard himself seems to have taken them in his stride. I suppose the hustings prepare you for anything."

"Yes, sir." Sloan braced himself and said, "I'm afraid there's yet another complication about the queremitte pellet."

"Don't tell me, Sloan," pleaded Leeyes theatrically. "Let me guess . . ."

Rightly interpreting this as a purely rhetorical remark, Detective Inspector Sloan forged on. "After the re-enactment at Mellamby Place the Society members sat down to a grand luncheon in the form of a medieval banquet."

"Ah," said Leeyes, "I know what that means, Sloan."

"You do, sir?" said Sloan, surprised.

"No forks," said the Superintendent. "They hadn't been invented."

"I wouldn't know about that, sir, but what I do know is——"

"And Charles Laughton throwing chicken legs over his shoulder and on to the rushes on the floor."

"Talking of chicken legs, sir," put in Sloan rather desperately, "someone seems to have been trying to put a hex on someone at Mellamby."

"As Henry VIII, of course, Sloan, unless you're too young to remember?"

"Quite so, sir," Sloan sighed. "At Mellamby it was Adrian Dungey as Henry III. He and Simon de Montfort sat at the top table with the Member of Parliament, who made a speech."

"Ha! And what did our revered Member have to say at Mellamby?"

"I don't know, sir. I was more concerned with what they had to eat after the battle."

"Quite right," said Leeyes warmly. "Always more important. What was it?"

Sloan consulted his notebook. "Mortrews de fleyssh, Brewet, Pheasant, and Blamanger."

"Strewth!" exclaimed Leeyes.

"The Curate read Medieval History at Oxford and wanted them to get it right. They made him Pantler."

"Go on, Sloan, tell me. I can't bear the suspense."

"First cousin to a butler, sir."

"That's what I thought," he said unfairly. "What did they drink?"

"Home-made mead, sir. And in between each course they had something called a subtlety to clear the palate."

Leeyes muttered something inaudible.

Sloan hurried on. "The important thing from our point of view, sir, is that Bertram Rauly—the owner of the whole outfit—had a bit of an accident at the banquet."

"Too much mead?" suggested Leeyes solicitously, "or a surfeit of lampreys?"

"Some lead shot in the pheasant," said Sloan. "Or that's what he thought. He broke a tooth."

"I'm very sorry having to trouble you again, Mrs. Ottershaw," said Detective Inspector Sloan. The two policemen were back in April Cottage at Mellamby.

"I wasn't doing anything," said Hazel Ottershaw listlessly.

"Quite so," said Sloan.

"My mother's got the children," the widow waved a hand round the sitting room, "and it's funny but there doesn't seem anything to do any more. Nothing important, anyway." She smiled wanly. "Which is silly when you come to think about it, isn't it?"

Detective Inspector Sloan nodded sympathetically.

"Because Alan was away so much that you'd think it would be the same as if he was only back in Lasserta." Her voice fell away. "Only it isn't."

"No, Madam. Nothing's the same any more." It never was after a spouse died. Even he, Christopher Dennis Sloan, still happily married, knew that. Even if the poet was notoriously silent on what happened after the Moving Finger had writ. The author of *Omar Khayyám* had dwelt more on the fact that nothing could lure it back to cancel half a line.

And they all knew that.

"Everything's different," said the new widow, a note of surprise still in her voice. "Everything."

"Just so, Madam."

"People have been very kind, though," she murmured. "Very kind."

"I'm afraid, Madam," said Sloan, "that you are going to think me very unkind . . ."

She looked up at him. "I don't understand, Inspector."

"It's not easy to explain."

"What isn't?" There was a sudden sharp note in her voice now.

"We want you to do something for us."

"For the police?"

"Please."

"Of course." She sat up quite straight and braced her shoulders. "Naturally, Inspector, anything I can do to help the police, I will. Although I must confess I don't see in what way I could—"

Detective Inspector Sloan reached into an inside pocket. "Your late husband worked in Lasserta, which, Madam, as you don't need me to tell you, is one of the more politically sensitive parts of the world."

She opened her hands expressively. "The Middle East . . ."

"Exactly." Sloan didn't know the degree of difficulty and danger that divided a trouble-spot from a running sore, but his mind was on other things anyway.

"It's always been like that, Inspector."

"Yes, Madam." Sloan kept his eye on Mrs. Ottershaw's face. "Your late husband also worked for a company mining a politically sensitive metal."

She nodded: no company wife needed telling that. "Queremitte."

"I understand you told the doctors at the hospital who were treating your husband that his unexpected return had had something to do with some difficulty in Lasserta."

She raised her head up and braced her shoulders. "That's what he told me, Inspector, when he got back from Wadeem."

"Some sudden difficulty?"

"Oh, yes. Very sudden. I didn't know anything about it until he arrived back home."

"But he didn't tell you exactly what it was about?"

She passed a hand in front of her eyes. "He said it was trouble of some kind after a road accident."

"That all?"

"Yes. He told me his firm were anxious that he shouldn't discuss the details so——"

"So he didn't?"

She looked up, surprised. "Of course not, Inspector."

"As it happens," said Sloan formally, "his firm has confirmed this."

"Then what can I do for you?" she asked, slightly more distant in her manner too.

"At some time during the Sunday morning—the day that he died —the Anglo-Lassertan Mineral Company recorded a message from your husband on their answering machine."

"From Alan?" This was patently news to Alan Ottershaw's widow. She paled.

"They say so."

Hazel Ottershaw's head came up with a jerk. "What did it say?"

"You didn't know about it, then, Madam?"

"No . . . no, I didn't even know he'd rung them. Mind you, Inspector," she recovered herself quickly and essayed a small smile, "I was pretty busy that morning what with the children and getting ready for the re-enactment. I might have been upstairs when Alan telephoned them."

"So," ventured Sloan carefully, "you didn't know what he had been going to say to them?"

"No . . ." she said more slowly. "I didn't."

"And he didn't tell you afterwards that he had rung them?"

"No. No, he didn't. Not that there was a lot of time for chat that morning." She looked at him anxiously. "Is it important, then?"

Sloan didn't give Hazel Ottershaw a direct answer. Instead he said, "It would appear from what was on the tape of the answering machine that the call to the Anglo-Lassertan Mineral Company from your husband originated in a public telephone kiosk."

That did startle Hazel Ottershaw.

"I didn't know about that . . . But . . . So . . ." She struggled for speech but gave up, and stiffened and sat up very straight indeed.

"So?" Detective Inspector Sloan hadn't needed a lecturer in psychology to teach him the technique known as repetitive listening. He had found out when he was still virtually a boy on the beat that the best way of getting anyone to go on talking was to repeat after them the last words that they had spoken themselves. This practice of echoing was even more effective in getting people to go on talking than encouraging nods or enthusiastic agreement.

It didn't work with Hazel Ottershaw. Not this time. She shook her head and said, "Nothing, Inspector. I wasn't going to say anything."

"The Anglo-Lassertan Mineral Company recorded the message," said Sloan smoothly.

Hazel Ottershaw said nothing.

"And acted on it."

"So?" she said interrogatively, running her tongue over lips that appeared now to be dry.

"So we would like you to confirm the voice on the message tape as being that of your husband."

"I see." She moistened her lips again. "Yes, of course. If it is," she added.

"Naturally," said Sloan. "Crosby, the tape-recorder, please."

He watched the Detective Constable set up the machine, one half of his mind automatically registering Hazel Ottershaw's body language, the other half well back in his own life-time.

When he, Christopher Dennis Sloan, had been a callow youth he had got caught up with attending a Brains Trust at his mother's church. Only as a member of the audience, of course—public speaking was neither his forte nor his ambition. A kindly clergyman had found adult foils for those who did favour this form of Chinese torture and set the stage for the occasion.

He had also set the questions.

One—or, rather, its answer—had seared its way into Sloan's burgeoning adolescent consciousness.

If, the Chairman had asked his Panel, you could hear again any voice from the past, whose would it be?

Jesus Christ had been the first to be suggested, and William Shakespeare next.

The schoolmaster in the team had opted for the Greek Demosthenes. He would, wouldn't he, someone had muttered, even though a great orator was a logical choice in the circumstances.

The answer that had shaken a younger Sloan had come from the Mayor—the most self-confident and successful of all the Panel members: sixty if he was a day, and known throughout the town as a stern man of business. "My mother's," the hard-bitten Mayor had mumbled in a low voice, his complexion going a dull turkey-cock red.

"Ready, sir," murmured Crosby. "Shall I switch it on?"

"I'm sorry having to do this, Madam," said Sloan.

Hazel Ottershaw's face took on a rigid expression from which all emotion had been expunged and as the cassette started to turn she braced her shoulders as if readying herself for a body blow.

Even Sloan had found it eerie listening to the voice of a man so recently dead. He knew that words spoken *in articulo mortis*—at the point of death—had a special significance in law. And in religion, too, come to that. They were deemed likely to be true because it was believed that the safety of a man's immortal soul overrode his fear of other men's justice.

But that proposition required that the dying man knew as he spoke the words that he was going to die.

Alan Ottershaw hadn't known on that Sunday morning when he telephoned the Anglo-Lassertan Mineral Company that he would be dead by evening.

Not as far as Sloan knew anyway.

And yet Ottershaw had spoken them like a man condemned.

His voice had been flat and formal as he had left his message with his London office. Its import was simple. He had thought a lot about the man he had killed in the road accident in Lasserta and wanted to go back to Gatt-el-Abbas to face the music. He felt that this was the right and proper course of action on his part. He hadn't —and at this point a note of earnestness came into his voice—realised that coming home to try to evade Lassertan justice would lead to so many complications. He hoped that the firm would arrange his immediate return to the Sheikhdom whatever the consequences . . .

His widow was listening intently, sitting with her head bent forwards and downwards at an attentive angle which somehow contrived to obscure her face from the full view of the two policemen. Nothing, though, could hide her sagged shoulders or disguise the fine tremor present in her hands. Sloan had once read that the painter, Renoir, had always held that the hands revealed more of the person than the face and, policeman that he was, he kept his eye on Hazel Ottershaw's hands now. She, too, must have perceived the little shake there because she suddenly clenched them into tight fists that stayed still.

Crosby switched off the tape-recorder while Alan Ottershaw was still speaking. Sloan waited for her to say something. Hazel Ottershaw, though, her face drained and white, seemed to be having difficulty in formulating words. She visibly struggled for speech but no sound came and in the end she only nodded at him.

He still waited for what she had to say.

It seemed to the policeman to be important to know what it would be. Alan Ottershaw's widow had said that she hadn't known about the message on the tape and since it had been conveyed audibly on a public payphone that might well be true. Before she—or, indeed, Sloan—had known about the telephone call to the Anglo-Lassertan Mineral Company she had insisted to him that her husband had come back from his talk with the Member of Parliament reassured.

And yet the Member of Parliament had told the two policemen that he had promised to do all he could to prevent Alan Ottershaw being sent back to Lasserta by his employers or extradited by the Lassertans to stand trial.

He had said that this had been what the mining engineer had wanted him to do, but urgently.

A Member of Parliament—no, two Members of Parliament—who seemed to be the targets for something sinister, too.

Her face still working, Hazel Ottershaw said painfully, "Yes, Inspector, that was Alan's voice."

"Do you know what it was, madam, that made your husband decide to go back to Lasserta?" From where Sloan sat at the moment, that, whatever it was, had been an overnight conversion.

She obviously didn't trust herself to speak. She just shook her head.

Sloan still kept his eye on her face as he reached inside the wallet of papers which he had brought with him. He took out a photograph and handed it to Hazel Ottershaw, asking, "Do you recognise this man?"

"It's Hamer Morenci, Inspector." Her voice was little more than a whisper. "He's the head of Alan's firm. He spoke at Alan's funeral."

"We know about that," said Sloan. "What we want to know is whether you saw him at Mellamby the day your husband died."

"No," she said at once. Then "Yes . . ." Her face crumpled. "Oh, I don't know . . ."

FOURTEEN

For Even the Purest
Delight May Pall

"YES," said Adrian Dungey much more positively.

At least the next person to look at the same picture appeared to know his own mind.

Which Hazel Ottershaw hadn't.

"Yes, Inspector," repeated the young veterinarian. "I'm almost sure I saw the man in this photograph here in Mellamby on the day of the battle and I'll tell you why."

Detective Inspector Sloan looked at him encouragingly. Touches of corroborative detail were always welcome additions to any statement given in a police context.

"Because," said Dungey, "when the Chairman of Anglo-Lassertan got up to speak at poor old Alan's funeral, I had a definite feeling that I'd seen his face before somewhere but at the time I couldn't think where." He tapped the photograph of Hamer Morenci. "And this explains it. It must have been at the Battle of Lewes."

"Can you remember, sir, exactly where you might have seen him on the day of the re-enactment?" A certain obstinate refusal to be party to the play-acting of the Camulos Society prevented Sloan from using the word "battlefield." "It might help us if you could."

The two policemen were sitting in the veterinary surgeon's consulting room whither they had been ushered after a brief delay in the waiting room. The vet's receptionist had slipped them in ahead of an Alsatian dog with a sore paw and after a tortoiseshell Persian cat whose problems were not apparent to a lay observer.

The veterinary practice kept some budgerigars in a bird cage in the waiting room to distract unwell cats, presumably on the same principle that Sloan's dentist had a goldfish tank in his waiting room to occupy the attention of his anxious patients. The Alsatian dog had taken a keen interest in the Persian cat, the cat had watched the budgerigars, and Sloan had run his eye over his notes. There had been nothing but old magazines to amuse Detective Constable Crosby, which was a pity because he was easily bored.

Adrian Dungey shook his head at Sloan's question. "Sorry, Inspector, I'm not sure that I can. You've got to remember that it was a real mêlée that day from the middle of the morning onwards—from the moment when church came out until the end of the afternoon."

"So we understand," said Sloan neutrally. Going to church before a battle was a very old tradition indeed. He remembered that somewhere in Sir Thomas Malory's *Morte d'Arthur* a knight—was it the great and good Sir Lancelot himself?—had actually kept vigil there the night before a conflict. He gave himself a little mental shake: he must remember that his job was usually with the small and the bad. "Go on," he said.

"It was bound to be a bit of a muddle," Dungey responded, "seeing that it was a cross between a pageant and a beanfeast." He jerked his head. "To say nothing of all and sundry being welcome to come and watch—old Bertram Rauly's nothing if not generous."

"Something for everyone, you might say," observed Sloan.

"Even Hamer Morenci," added Crosby.

"I suppose," said Dungey, frowning, "that his boss might have come down to Mellamby to see Alan about work. After all, he was the head of his firm and there did seem to have been something very odd indeed about Alan's coming home so suddenly."

"Indeed, sir?" Detective Inspector Sloan's intonation was at its silkiest.

"I didn't get to talk to him about it myself, Inspector. No time. Besides, he might not have told me. None of my business anyway, of course."

"Ah."

"Hazel might know."

"I'm told," ventured Sloan, "that you had something of a fight with the—er—deceased yourself."

Adrian Dungey's face lit up. "I'll say, Inspector! Alan was in magnificent form then. I had to watch my footwork, I can tell you . . ." His eagerness crumpled away. "The doctors thought he might have overdone it, you know."

Sloan nodded.

"The fighting coming on top of the jet-lag." He essayed a weak smile. "A bit like poor old King Harold force-marching it to Hastings to meet William the Conqueror straight after coping with Harold Hardrada and Tostig at Stamford Bridge."

"Just so," murmured Sloan. No one could say Adrian Dungey wasn't as far into war games as Bertram Rauly and the little Major.

"To say nothing of the change in temperature."

"Very taxing, I'm sure, sir." Sloan decided the vet was talking about England and Lasserta now and not Stamford Bridge and Hastings: and Crosby did not appear to care.

"But it was a grand fight all the same."

Sloan made a note. Shakespeare had been right about old battles being remembered with advantages. All old battles.

"Although naturally I deeply regretted it afterwards in case all the extra exertion had contributed to his death."

"Naturally, sir."

"I wasn't to know, you see."

"No." Sloan took his part in the coda of contrition.

"Moreover we all knew that King Henry III fought like a Trojan at the real thing."

Crosby smirked. "What you might call a Battle Royal."

"No," said Detective Inspector Sloan, policeman.

"No," said Adrian Dungey, veterinary surgeon and wargame enthusiast.

"No?" said Crosby, looking slightly bewildered.

"Battle Royal," said Dungey hortatively, "is the opposite of single-handed combat. It's a general squabble."

"A free-for-all?" Crosby brightened. It was the sort of engagement he favoured himself.

"The term," contributed Detective Inspector Sloan out of his own experience, "also applies to cock-fighting, of which crime, Crosby,

I'm happy to say, we do not have enough in this manor for you to have seen."

"Not a lot of it about," agreed the vet. "Not now."

Sloan came back to the purpose of his enquiry with the constancy of a self-righting Russian doll. "This fight you had with the deceased, sir . . ."

"Yes, Inspector?"

"Whereabouts on the—er—battlefield did it take place?"

Adrian Dungey relaxed. "Near the foot of the ruined tower of the Motte, Inspector. You see, as far as we can establish, King Henry III stayed around Lewes Castle all through the battle until he was taken prisoner." His boyish eagerness reasserted itself as he talked. "There's a lot of verse about the Battle of Lewes, you know."

"No, sir," said Sloan. "I didn't."

Dungey promptly declaimed:

> A little bande arounde the Kyng,
> Unflinching kept their grounde.

"Did they?" said Sloan heavily.

Undeterred, Dungey carried on quoting:

> But all in vain—th'exulting foe
> Rush'd onwards on his ire—
> And Henrye and his faithful friendes
> Unwillinglye retire.

"And after your encounter with the deceased, sir?" The only verse that came immediately to Sloan's mind was from a Scottish ballad:

> But I hae dream'd a dreary dream,
>   Beyond the Isle of Skye,
> I saw a dead man win a fight,
>   And I think that man was I.

From all accounts what went for the Earl of Douglas at the Battle of Otterbourne had gone for Alan Ottershaw too.

Dungey said easily, "Oh, I just joined in the general fighting until the Battle Commander called the field to rest at half-past twelve."

"Time for din-dins, was it?" said Crosby, demolishing the carefully contrived atmosphere of the High Middle Ages at a stroke.

Detective Inspector Sloan hastily changed tack, asking the vet, "Were you round about the tower when the piece of masonry came down?"

Dungey's eyes narrowed, his manner instantly sober again. "I was. And I shan't forget that in a hurry."

Crosby stirred. "Did it fall or was it pushed?"

"I can't tell you that." He shook his shoulders slightly. "All I can tell you, gentlemen, is that it was a very near miss. Poor old Peter Corbishley damn nearly had his chips, I assure you. Not that it shook him—or, if it did, he didn't let it show."

Sloan nodded. There were, he knew, public figures so in control of their own image that they could almost override reality.

"Major Puiver started to climb up to the parapet—there's a stairway up inside the tower—but by the time he got even halfway up whoever had hefted the stone over—if they had, of course——"

"If they had," agreed Sloan.

"—wasn't there any more." Adrian Dungey shrugged his shoulders. "But it was that sort of day. A lot of comings and goings."

"More's the pity," said Crosby, who liked things easy.

"The death and dislocation of war," quoted Sloan gravely.

"I thought," said Dungey, "that I'd caught a glimpse of the Figure of Death up there myself while Alan and I were fighting down below, but I may have been wrong."

"Death," said Sloan, conscious of sounding rather like an Old Testament prophet, "seems to have been everywhere that day."

"The Major told me he thought he recognised the man's walk. Seen it before somewhere, he said, but he couldn't be sure where." Dungey shrugged his shoulders. "He couldn't place him, anyway, and neither could anyone else. And, of course," it was the vet's turn to sound profound, "Death didn't speak."

"As silent as the grave, was he?" said Crosby jauntily. He seemed to have cheered up suddenly because he waved a playful hand in the vet's direction and said, "Considering how little a tongue weighs, it's funny how few people can hold it, isn't it?"

TED SHEARD, the Labour Member of Parliament for the West Berebury Division of Calleshire, was as hard-working and as committed as Peter Corbishley. Where they differed was in style: Robin Good-fellow had nothing on Ted Sheard.

His Party Headquarters were over in the west of Berebury amidst the rows of little artisans' dwellings built to house the influx of railway workers to the town of more than a century before. He ran a constituency surgery there, and from this unpromising power-base waged unrelenting war on unfeeling bureaucracies, dilatory national bodies, and a judicial system that, in his view, fed on the hopelessly incompetent. On every possible platform he campaigned for a Brave New World for society's casualties.

The Member of Parliament for West Berebury, like the Member for East Berebury, couldn't for the life of him think why anyone should send either him or Peter Corbishley death threats.

"Let's hope it isn't for the life of you, sir," said Detective Inspector Sloan soberly. "Tell me about them."

"They started coming through the post after Easter," said the Member, "and they addressed me as Taurus."

"As in the Zodiac?"

"Precisely, Inspector."

"Signed?"

"By someone calling himself Scorpio." He paused. "Or herself. Or themselves. It was a drawing."

"The Scorpion," said Crosby intelligently.

"To begin with, they were just simple messages like 'Your hour is come' and 'Death is nigh.' They sort of worked their way up to live scorpions. By way of a butterfly, actually."

"A butterfly?" said Detective Constable Crosby, interested in the oddness.

"Well, that's what I thought it was at first." Sheard grinned. "Turned out to be a Death's Head Moth. I got the spike after that all right. Until then I thought I might have had some of the animal rights campaigners after me." He looked shrewdly at Sloan. "They get up to all sorts of things."

"We know," said Sloan. "We know."

"All in a day's work, I said to myself, at first," remarked Sheard, "hate-mail, although I must say that the letters put my girl in a bit of a two and eight." He shrugged his shoulders. "I know you can't please all the people all the time but—"

"But some of them you can't please any of the time," finished the policeman for him out of the depths of his own experience.

"I thought I'd just got on the wrong side of some nutter although there was no other message with them. That was to begin with, you understand."

"So things got worse?" deduced Sloan.

"I'll say," responded the Member. He was a large cheerful man who must have found it quite difficult to look down-hearted whatever the circumstances. "One morning I found a socking great effigy of myself swinging on my front gate. It couldn't have been there long because it was the morning after a late-night sitting of the House and I only got back from Westminster just in time for an early breakfast."

"Nasty," observed Sloan.

"It's a funny feeling, Inspector, I can tell you, cutting down a dummy figure of yourself."

"Like a goose grazing on your grave," contributed Crosby helpfully. "You know, when your flesh goes pimply all of a sudden."

"And funnier still," said Ted Sheard grimly, "when you find that a meat skewer has been stuck through its heart."

"Voodoo . . ." said Crosby.

"It doesn't make sense someone wanting both Members of Parliament dead," said Sheard. "One or the other and it might be politics. But not both."

"Who do? . . ." chanted Crosby.

"I thought at first it might be the university students up to their usual tricks, but then I got an invitation to talk to them at Almstone College and they were all right on the night."

"You do . . ." finished Crosby.

"Crosby!" admonished Sloan.

"Well, that's what they used to do in the old days, wasn't it?" said the Constable defensively. "When they wanted someone to die they stuck a pin through the heart of a wax image. When they wanted someone just to suffer they stuck it where they wanted it to hurt."

"Thank you very much, Constable," said the Member feelingly before Sloan could speak. "Actually, I got that far on my own and then when I compared notes with Corbishley I thought I'd better let you people know."

"Quite right, sir," said Sloan. "Quite right. And you confirm that all these threats only indicated the one thing that the writer wanted you to do?"

"Die," said Sheard tersely. "Oh, I got the message all right. Somebody out there means me to keel over and turn my toes up, though don't ask me why."

"And you've never had any death threats before?"

"Not anonymously through the post, Inspector."

There was something in the way that Ted Sheard spoke which made Sloan look up sharply.

The Member grinned and said impishly, "I've been getting them regularly for years from someone else."

"Sir?"

"My doctor."

"Ah."

"He threatens me with death every time he sees me."

"Oh?"

"Makes me stand on the oldest biofeedback machine of them all and then starts wringing his hands."

"What's that machine then, sir?" asked Sloan, suspecting a catch.

"The weighing scales. And," Sheard went on genially, "then he says I must give up eating, drinking, smoking and working."

"Or else?" said Sloan, entering into the spirit of the exchange.

"Or else a by-election, Inspector. And since the first duty of a politician is to be re-elected that wouldn't do at all. He thinks I should take more exercise, too, but then he's not in politics." He frowned. "Well, only medical politics."

"And you have no idea why anyone should be gunning for you and Mr. Corbishley?" asked Sloan. At least neither Member showed any sign of persecution mania: which was a help to a hard-pressed police force. Paranoia was difficult for anyone to deal with.

"I daresay we've both got enemies, Inspector," said Sheard philosophically. "All God's parliamentary chillen got enemies."

"Except, sir, that it would seem to be a plague on both your houses, so to speak." You couldn't beat the Bard for aptness.

"*Rouge et noir,* Inspector, you might say," agreed Sheard slyly, "rather than *Rogue ou noir.*"

"Sir?"

"Do you play roulette, Inspector?"

"No, sir. I find I get enough excitement in my daily work, thank you."

"I didn't mean Russian roulette, Inspector."

"Neither did I, sir."

"*Rouge et noir* would be backing both sides of the table. Red or black is the usual way of playing."

"I take your point, sir," said Sloan, suppressing a strong desire to quote W. S. Gilbert's couplet about every child born alive being either a little Liberal or a little Conservative. Instead he said, "Have you ever heard of the Sheikhdom of Lasserta, sir?"

A remarkably discerning look overtook the Parliamentarian's professional geniality. He said quietly, "I've heard of queremitte, Inspector, if that's what you want to know."

"Yes, sir."

"A very valuable product indeed," advanced the Member.

"So I understand, sir."

"It's ore has been of great interest to various Parliamentary Select Committees," mused Ted Sheard. "I serve on one of them myself as it happens." He looked up quickly and said in quite a different tone of voice, "But you already knew that, Inspector, didn't you?"

Sloan coughed. "Yes, sir. As it happens, I did."

"You'll have done your homework before you came to see me." It was a statement, not a question.

"Quite so, sir."

Sheard twisted his lips. "To go back to roulette, Inspector."

"Sir?"

"I should say for a start that anything to do with queremitte would up the stakes in any game you care to mention."

"So would I, sir," agreed Sloan softly.

"An altogether different ball game from live scorpions, gentlemen, in spite of the Parliamentary overtones."

"I don't think I know about those, sir."

"The Old Testament, Inspector." The Member stretched his arms outwards and upwards. "Don't look so surprised. I used to be a lay preacher before I went in to politics and scorpions rang a Biblical bell." In a fine declamatory style and in a rich intonation designed to carry, Ted Sheard delivered the words "My Father has chastised you with whips, but I will chastise you with scorpions. First Book of Kings, Chapter Twelve."

Crosby stirred. "I don't see what——"

"We have Whips, Constable," he explained gently, "in the Houses of Parliament. To see that we vote."

"AND WHAT we have to remember about the Old Testament, Crosby," said Detective Inspector Sloan as he settled himself back into the passenger seat of the police car, "is that Exodus follows Genesis a long way before you get to the First Book of Kings."

"Yes, sir."

Sloan hunched his shoulders forward. "And all this case is doing at the moment is getting more complicated." He pulled his notebook out. "Remind me to ask Peter Corbishley if they've asked him to speak at Almstone College too."

"Yes, sir." Detective Constable Crosby changed the gears of the engine upwards as if rehearsing for the Mille Miglia. "How come that character we've just met knows about both roulette and the Bible? That's not natural."

"I expect he's what they call a polymath. And his name, Crosby, let me remind you is Edward Montague Hopperton Sheard, although I think he likes to be called Ted."

"If you ask me," said Crosby, taking a corner as if a race depended on it, "I think he likes to be called to dinner."

FIFTEEN

And Power Must Fail

DR. DABBE, the consultant pathologist, was hard at work when Detective Inspector Sloan and Detective Constable Crosby were shown into the mortuary. He gave the two policemen a friendly wave of greeting and called out, "Won't keep you a moment, gentlemen. Just tying a few loose ends, you might say."

Crosby averted his eyes.

"So are we, Doctor," said Sloan evenly. "If we can."

"At the moment," contributed Crosby with a wholly artificial jauntiness, "we seem to have as many as a packet of spaghetti."

The pathologist busied himself for another few minutes over something dreadfully inert on an operating table, and then he straightened his back and spoke to his assistant. "There we are, Burns, all done. He's fit for an identity parade now. Even his worst enemy would know him."

The perennially silent Burns nodded.

Dr. Dabbe turned his back on his assistant, motioning him to undo the strings of his gown. He spoke, though, to Sloan. "I'm very sorry to have to tell you, Inspector, that this is going to be one of those times when the old rubric about pathologists doesn't run true."

"What's that, Doctor?" asked Sloan, mystified.

"As you may know, Inspector, the physician knows everything and does nothing." He turned his head. "Thank you, Burns, that will do nicely."

Sloan didn't know a lot about physicians and their laissez-faire attitude to life. And death.

"And the surgeon," quoted Dabbe, "knows nothing and does everything. Burns, my gloves."

Sloan had always been afraid of that. Activists, that was what surgeons were.

Dabbe grinned. "You don't need me to tell you anything about psychiatrists, do you now, Sloan?"

"No, Doctor."

"They know nothing and do nothing," he said briefly. "My cap, Burns. Catch."

Sloan agreed with this statement with a ready fervour while Dr. Dabbe moved towards the washhand basin in the corner.

"As for the pathologists . . ." Dr. Dabbe paused.

Detective Constable Crosby leaned forward curiously. "What about the pathologists then?"

Dr. Dabbe halted in the act of scrubbing his hands. "Ah, usually the pathologist knows everything but too late to do anything. Burns, a clean towel, please."

"Not in this case?" Sloan had got the message all right.

" 'Fraid not, Inspector. This pathologist only knows that the ashes you brought here are of *homo sapiens.*"

"Human," said Crosby intelligently.

"Not something played for by opposing cricket teams," agreed Dabbe gravely.

"Or someone's favourite pet," said Sloan. Luston's Motorway Man—the trick perpetrated on his opposite number at Luston—had bitten deep.

"Pure Sam McGee," Dabbe assured him.

"Pardon, Doctor?"

"Shame on you, Sloan," chided the pathologist. "I'm sure you've heard of 'The Shooting of Dan McGrew.' "

"Yes, Doctor," said Sloan evenly.

"Dangerous Dan McGrew?" said Crosby.

"None other," said Dabbe. "Well, 'The Cremation of Sam McGhee' comes from the same stable. Don't you remember:

There are strange things done in the midnight sun
   By the men who moil for gold;
The Arctic trails have their secret tales
   That would make your blood run cold.

"No, Doctor," said Sloan truthfully.

"Ah, well," said Dabbe generously, "you can't know everything." He brightened. "I can tell you—Geiger counters being what they are —that the person to whom these ashes belonged hadn't been subject to irradiation." He looked at Sloan. "I don't suppose, though, that's a lot of help."

"Not at this stage," said Sloan politely.

Dabbe ushered the two policemen through into his office and motioned them into the chairs there. "I got your call about Bertram Rauly's broken tooth and I'm afraid I can't even help you there."

"We couldn't afford to overlook any possibility, Doctor." That, after all, was what police work was all about.

"I can't tell you if what broke it was a queremitte pellet and, which is worse, I can't tell you either if the queremitte pellet that did get into the deceased had been ingested or introduced into his body through the skin."

Sloan wasn't surprised. "After all, nobody knows for sure where-abouts in his body it was, do they? Not now."

"Nor do we know," the pathologist reminded him, "whether or not the queremitte pellet had anything to do with his death."

"No . . ."

"Or, if it did, whether or not the aforementioned pellet did contain a noxious substance."

"No, Doctor . . ." Sloan had to admit that what they did not know would fill a policeman's notebook. He made a mental note to remind himself to check if the combatants of the Camulos Society had partaken of the spirituous equivalent of the stirrup-cup before the battle—or did they have lemon slices at half-time?

"And if it did," continued Dabbe, "whether or not it was taken by the deceased deliberately."

"Suicide?" exclaimed Sloan involuntarily. "I hadn't considered that."

"We can't afford to overlook any possibility, Inspector." Dabbe frowned. "I must say if I had to choose between that and death by a thousand cuts in Lasserta I might opt for *felo de se* myself."

"But Ottershaw didn't have to go back," said Sloan before he realised that this was another aspect of the case he hadn't really thought through properly. That telephone call to the Anglo-Lassertan offices was very nearly as mysterious as the pellet in the ashes.

"Your pigeon, Sloan, not mine." Restored to his everyday clothing, the pathologist looked almost human. "I take it you've looked into the availability of queremitte?"

"Not a lot of help to be had there, Doctor. We've established that the pellet in the ashes had been made out of the small samples of the stuff that the firm itself distributes to schools and universities and so forth for teaching and experimental research purposes. And to potential customers."

"Our Army," said Dabbe cheerfully, "and I sincerely hope to nobody else's."

Sloan ignored this tempting by-way. "These samples are spool-shaped and hollow. They even look a bit like shot. All anyone would have to do would be to cut one in half and seal off the open end with something soluble after they'd put something in it."

"I thought it was a hard metal and that was why the Army liked it," remarked Dabbe.

"They put it with something else—they don't want to tell us what —for what they call its enhancing effect." Even the Services had Public Relations Officers these days.

"Synergism," said the doctor.

"If you say so, Doctor," said Sloan. "Anyway, that's where the great hardness comes in."

"Makes a change from a platinum-iridium alloy, in any case," said the pathologist. "Fired by an umbrella-gun," he added as Sloan's expression remained uncomprehending. "With a fatal dose of ricin in it."

"Ah, yes, of course, Doctor." A precedent would make its mark in every discipline. "I'd forgotten that . . ."

There was a moment of quietness in the pathologist's room and then Dr. Dabbe spoke again, this time more diffidently. "There is, of course, another approach to the problem raised by the death of Ottershaw."

"Yes, Doctor?" Sloan was all in favour of lateral thinking.

"Starting, Sloan, with what is known about the deceased's last illness."

"A heart attack," said Crosby.

"Exactly." Dr. Dabbe turned towards the Detective Constable. "We already know, for example, don't we, that the deceased wasn't done to death with ox-bones like poor St. Alphege."

"Yes . . ." agreed Crosby with caution.

Sloan said nothing. Lateral thinking could obviously go a long way round to get to wherever it was going.

"After all," continued the pathologist, "two duly authorised registered medical practitioners certified that Alan John Ottershaw had died from a heart attack."

Sloan's expression became even more cautious than Crosby's. He could metaphorically hear the sound of deep calling to deep as professional solidarity raised its ugly head. Doctors always hung together so that they weren't sued separately.

"While it is, of course, theoretically possible," carried on Dr. Dabbe, "that two serious errors of medical judgement were made, it is, you must agree, somewhat unlikely."

"What about collusion?" asked Crosby, much perkier now that he was out of the mortuary.

"That's your pigeon, too," countered Dabbe, "but to whose benefit? No, what I have been doing is looking at the problem from the other end." He pulled a sheet of paper towards him. "Let us suppose for the sake of argument that the pellet itself did not cause death."

Sloan waited, attentive but silent.

"Injury," amplified the pathologist, "or even metallic poisoning, would not have given rise to those signs."

Sloan nodded.

"But suppose that a substance contained in the pellet did."

"Like the ricin," said Crosby.

Detective Inspector Sloan leaned forward. "You mean, Doctor, that the heart failure might have been the outcome of poisoning?"

"Precisely, Inspector, and yes, Constable. It is a theoretical possibility and therefore must be considered."

"Scorpions?" asked Sloan swiftly.

"Not scorpions," responded Dabbe. "Their sting is painful but not usually fatal."

"What, then?"

"Sting-rays, venomous fishes, some newts, the kokoi frog . . ."

"In Calleshire?" said Crosby sceptically.

"Someone found some scorpions for Ted Sheard," said Sloan quietly. He reached for his notebook. This was something a policeman could get to grips with. "And what poisons would have that effect, Doctor?"

"The sympathomimetic agents."

Sloan subsided back into his chair without attempting to write anything down. He might have known that what the doctor would say wouldn't be simple. It seldom was.

Dabbe frowned. "All I can say is that it is a proposition that would account for both the pellet and the heart failure." He essayed a quick smile across his desk. "I wouldn't go to the stake for it, Sloan. It's only what the scientific people would call a tenuous hypothesis."

"These agents you mentioned, Doctor."

"Epinephrine and its group of related drugs."

The gardener in Sloan appreciated that drugs—like plants and people—came in families and had relations. The policeman in him took note that a working possibility of poisoning existed.

The pathologist squinted down at the sheet of paper on his desk and said with unusual care, "If we're talking about this sort of thing . . ."

"We are, aren't we?" said Crosby, suddenly alert.

"Then one would have to include the venoms, too."

Crosby brightened still further. "Arrow poisons, you mean, Doctor?"

Sloan had often wondered if the Detective Constable's reading had ever got beyond the comic-paper stage.

The answer had to be wrung out of the pathologist. "I'm afraid we can't rule them out," said Dr. Dabbe regretfully.

It was Detective Constable Crosby, though, who had the last word. "The evidence still doesn't amount to a hill of beans, does it?"

"WHERE HAVE WE GOT TO so far, Crosby?" asked Detective Inspector Sloan presently.

"The railway station, sir," responded the Constable from the driving seat of the police car and taking the question literally. "A bit to go yet to the police ditto."

Sloan tried again. "And what have we got so far in the little matter of Regina *versus* whoever killed Alan Ottershaw?" His lips tightened. "If they did, that is."

"An appetite," said Crosby with fervour. "I could eat a horse."

Detective Inspector Sloan, who had been trying not to dwell on the fact that his wife Margaret had promised him a home-made steak-and-kidney pudding for dinner, said, "We've got a pellet made of queremitte."

"And that's all we have got," responded Crosby morosely, "isn't it?"

"A queremitte pellet," continued Detective Inspector Sloan in a minatory way, "found in the cremated ashes of a man who comes home from abroad and dies two days later."

"Even that's not a lot, is it, sir?"

"We have also got an unconfirmed story—" meticulously Sloan corrected himself: "a story awaiting confirmation about a road accident that might or might not have been a genuine accident."

"In foreign parts, though," put in Crosby with a speed that would have done credit to Zeno himself.

"Where the victim of the road accident was already dead."

"It happens," said Crosby, quondam Traffic Division policeman, "all the time."

"And where the car driver, just before he himself dies—"

"Or is murdered," said Crosby changing gear.

"Or is murdered."

"In another country," said the xenophobe.

"In another country," echoed Sloan irritably, as always reminded by the phrase of a hymn whose meaning teased his mother. It began easily enough with "I vow to thee, my country"; it was the start of verse two which had always puzzled her. The first line of this was "And there's another country I've heard of long ago" and arguments about it invariably ended inconclusively with Mrs. Sloan senior saying, "I'm sure the author had Heaven in mind but why doesn't he say so?"

Detective Constable Crosby hadn't had Heaven in mind. Nor,

come to that, had Sloan. "In another country," he said heavily, "from which the car driver just before he dies declares himself—on a tape-recorder—willing, even anxious, to go back to Lasserta to—er —face the music. Although," he added because this seemed obscurely important, "his nearest and dearest do not appear to have known this."

If Sloan had been telling all this to the Assistant Chief Constable, that pillar of the Establishment would have said *"Floreat Etona"* or something similar at this point, he being a great man for a Latin tag.

All Detective Constable Crosby said was: "Doesn't make sense, does it, sir?"

The trouble was that he said it nonchalantly waving a hand in the air while overtaking a bus in the face of an oncoming lorry.

"We have also got," said Sloan between clenched teeth as the police car slid through a terrifyingly narrow gap, "a Member of Parliament who was being heckled by an unknown man, pursued by a character dressed as Death, being harassed by false calls to the ambulance service and narrowly escaping death from falling masonry." He drew breath and said with mounting acerbity, "Does any of that strike you as at all strange, Crosby?"

"Politics," responded Crosby dismissively. "All's fair in love, war, and politics."

Major Puiver would have said the Constable had got the battle order right: Bertram Rauly might not have done. He suspected that Ted Sheard would have said he had got it wrong. With a man like Peter Corbishley you would never know.

Sloan pursued his catalogue of what might or might not be evidence in what might or might not be a murder case. "We have also got another Member of Parliament of the opposite persuasion who is similarly being subjected to death threats and who is being sent live scorpions in his mail."

"Why not letter bombs?" asked Crosby. "Much more effective."

"Why not, indeed?" murmured Sloan seriously. "That's something we should think about."

"Sir, there's a good place to eat at——"

"And we've also got a highly eccentric landowner who has made no secret of the fact that he intends to burn down his historic house —it's almost a stately home—before he dies."

The philistine at the wheel of the police car said, "Well, it's his, isn't it?"

"Miss Finch would say you have no soul, Crosby."

Crosby said something almost as uncomplimentary about Miss Finch.

"The view of Miss Finch," said Detective Inspector Sloan, "is that Mellamby Place is part of the heritage of the nation."

"So are ruins," said Crosby ineluctably.

"And Miss Finch is one of the few people to have known that it wasn't Bertram Rauly who was in the costume of William de Wilton but the aforementioned Alan Ottershaw, deceased."

"Who may or may not have been murdered," said Crosby, driving triumphantly under an imaginary chequered flag at the entrance to the Police Station car park.

The message that awaited them could not have been more bizarre.

SIXTEEN

And the Pride Must Fall

"DO YOU MIND saying that again, sir?"

"Takes a bit of believing, Inspector, doesn't it?"

"Let's call it unusual, sir, shall we?" Both policemen were sitting in Peter Corbishley's house while the Member of Parliament repeated his story.

"I just went into Bert Swallow's barber's shop for my usual haircut."

Sloan nodded. The Member was a short-back-and-sides man if ever he saw one. He said, "By usual, sir, do you mean regular?"

"Good point, Inspector. Yes, I do. As near to the first of the month as I can get there."

"Rabbits," said Crosby.

"Parliamentary duties permitting, of course," continued the Member suavely.

"Quite so," said Sloan. There were some callings where getting your hair cut was part of a man's duty.

"Besides," the Member added drily, "my Agent likes it."

"Your appearance?" Sloan had always suspected that in politics it was the image that counted more than the man.

"My listening to what Bert has to say. He calls it keeping in touch with the grass roots."

"I understand," said Sloan austerely, "that taxi drivers have influence, too."

"My Agent sees Bert Swallow as the Calleshire equivalent of the man on the Clapham omnibus," said Corbishley. "Bert always gives me the—er—state-of-the-art view of current affairs." He hesitated. "That is one of the reasons why what has happened is so strange."

"So you were known to go there, sir, and roughly when."

"That is correct, Inspector."

"And when you went there you were known?"

"Oh, yes." The Member squared his shoulders. "It is still surprising in this day and age to learn that someone was willing, not to say anxious, to give Bert Swallow good money for keeping some of my hair after he had cut it and giving it to him."

"Very strange," conceded Sloan.

"But not funny. In fact it doesn't make sense."

"No."

"The man didn't want a lot of hair, Bert said, but he did need to be sure that it had come from my head."

"And what did Bert say to him?"

"That he's got a good sharp open razor by him and he'd be willing to use it if the man so much as set foot in his shop again. On his throat."

"Did he give you a description of the man?"

"Young and not very clean, he said, and in need of a haircut."

"He would say that, wouldn't he?" said Crosby.

"Clothes?" asked Sloan steadily.

"Jeans and an old coat," said Corbishley.

"No one that you can call to mind, sir?"

"No."

"Or have reason to suspect?"

"No."

"We'll go along and see Bert Swallow," undertook Sloan, "and ask him if he'd know this person again."

"Bert said he would recognise him by his walk," said Peter Corbishley.

"That's something," said Sloan. "Sir, there was something else we were going to ask you. Have you been invited to speak at the University of Calleshire lately?"

Peter Corbishley nodded. "Yes, indeed, Inspector. A group of Social Psychology students attending a seminar invited me to address them on the subject of 'Conflict and Stress.' Why?"

"I just wondered," said Sloan. He was struck by another thought. "One more thing, sir. When this character at the barber's asked Bert for your hair he didn't say anything to him about keeping quiet about it or not telling you, did he?"

"No."

"Odd, that, sir," said Sloan, "isn't it? When you come to think about it . . ."

The Member stared at him.

"It's all very well, Sloan," Superintendent Leeyes was saying half an hour later, "for you to list what may look like the material factors in the case."

"If there is a case." Sloan put in his usual caveat with a certain astringency.

"But what I want to know, Sloan," swept on Leeyes majestically, "is what you are going to do about it all."

"Well, sir," began Sloan cautiously, "first of all on the Parliamentary front, so to speak . . ."

"Yes?"

"I've sent Detective Constable Crosby to look into the availability in Calleshire of live scorpions."

Leeyes grunted. "He can't do a lot of harm doing that, I suppose."

"What is happening to those two Members of Parliament in the way of threats and so forth can't be coincidence. I'm sure of that."

"There's no such thing as coincidence in police work," pronounced Leeyes didactically. "I've told you that before, Sloan."

"So you have, sir." He hoped that the Superintendent would treat the remark as fact and not insubordination: he, Christopher Dennis Sloan, had his pension and a wife and son to think about. He hurried on. "They do, of course, belong to two different—two opposing—parties."

"That could be a blind, Sloan." Someone had once tried to explain the work of a true *agent provocateur* to the Superintendent and the concept had left its mark. "Just you watch it."

"Yes, sir." Grimly, he stuck to the point. "Neither Member of Parliament would appear to have felt really threatened or," he added fairly, "at least, if they have, they haven't acted running scared."

Leeyes sniffed. "Wouldn't do anything for their precious public images if they did, would it? Mind you, Sloan, if you ask me, half the electorate would vote for a dead ferret if it was wearing the right party colours."

"Quite so, sir." The History Man at Sloan's school had spent an unconscionable amount of teaching time on the passing of Lord Grey's Reform Bill of 1832. Even at this distance in time Sloan could see that the Bill couldn't have had an easy passage. Nothing, for instance, would have made a reformer out of Police Superintendent Leeyes.

"No representation without taxation, that's what I say, Sloan."

"Yes, sir." With the Boston Tea Party it had been the other way round, hadn't it?

"Mob rule," said Leeyes flatly. "That's what democracy is."

"I agree, sir, that it's what the word means," conceded Sloan. The Superintendent's brief attendance at an evening class on Parliamentary Government had ended abruptly with a "him or me" ultimatum from the tutor. Sloan swept on as quickly as he could: "Talking of political parties, sir, we've also checked out the neighbouring constituencies to East and West Calleshire in case they were having problems."

"Well?"

"Nobody threatened by anything worse than bad weather for their summer fêtes."

"So it's just our problem?" It didn't take too much to make the Superintendent feel hard done by.

"I'm afraid so, sir." Sloan glanced down at his notebook and said briskly, "I've also instituted a check of Calleshire and London theatrical costumiers."

"Death for hire?" intoned Leeyes morbidly.

"In a manner of speaking, sir. He must have got his clothes from somewhere. From Major Puiver's description, and Bertram Rauly's too, it sounded more of a professional job than the fancy dress that Miss Finch—she's the Wardrobe Mistress of Camulos Society, sir, if you remember—had cobbled together for everyone else."

"Wardrobe Mistress!" exclaimed Superintendent Leeyes. "Pah!"

"And I'm awaiting the Forensic Science Laboratory's report on the last threatening letter sent to Ted Sheard."

"At least they had the sense to keep that one."

Sloan coughed. "I understand, sir, that—er—stylistically all the letters would seem to have come from the same stable."

"Forensic over-reaching themselves as usual, I expect," said Leeyes uncharitably. "They never know when to stop."

"The report," ventured Sloan, "that all the letters were signed by drawings of the signs of the Zodiac may have influenced them."

"Kids' stuff," commented Leeyes richly.

"Those to Corbishley were addressed to Capricorn and signed Sagittarius and Sheard's to Taurus and signed Scorpio."

"Someone," said Leeyes, his head coming up like a foxhound scenting quarry, "has been reading their Rudyard Kipling."

"Sir?" Sloan suppressed a sigh. They had all hoped that the Superintendent had got his course on "Kipling—The Man and the Writer" out of his system by now.

"One of his strangest stories, Sloan, in which the Archer Kills the Goat and the Scorpion the Bull, is called 'The Children of the Zodiac.' Very difficult to understand, it was, although I told the lecturer——"

"I'm afraid," said Sloan, "the fact that this last letter was received after Alan Ottershaw died may indicate that the whole business of the attempted intimidation of the two Members of Parliament is unconnected with his death."

"Or it may not," retorted Leeyes unhelpfully. "Especially if this chap Sheard's being on the Parliamentary Select Committee looking into the purchasing arrangements for queremitte comes into it."

"I was coming to that, sir." Sloan looked up. "Is there any chance of our finding out?"

Leeyes' hollow laughter echoed round his office. "You'll be a better man than most, Gunga Din, if you can do that while they're still sitting. Unless you go and listen to the evidence yourself. You should know by now, Sloan, that Select Committees are creatures of procedure."

"But——"

"—and power." Leeyes grimaced. "Power to send for persons, papers and records if they want 'em. You thought only the courts could do that, Sloan, didn't you?"

Sloan hadn't thought about that at all.

"Well, Parliament's the highest court of all the land and don't you forget it."

"No, sir."

Leeyes grunted. "And a Parliamentary Select Committee's got the right—right, mind you, Sloan—to summon any British subject and make him cease his proper employment and come posting up to Westminster to give evidence before them."

"So . . ."

"All that matters to the House of Commons," said Leeyes, who had always taken the view that Guy Fawkes was a much maligned man, "is what the Select Committee says in their Report and if you can get a squeak out of anyone before it's published I'd be very surprised." He sniffed. "No precedent for it or something. But," he added graciously, "don't let me stop you trying."

"No, sir," said Sloan stolidly.

"What about the other Member? Peter Corbishley. Is there any connection between him and this precious metal?"

"It's not a prec——" began Sloan, and stopped. He thought precious metals were something else but couldn't be sure.

Not now.

Not here.

For all he knew, queremitte was something to be valued above rubies.

Like a virtuous woman.

"The Government's carrying on as if it is," said Leeyes unanswerably. "Otherwise they wouldn't be wanting to know why the Ministry of Defence Procurement is spending so much money on the stuff, would they?"

"No, sir."

"And what about a link with queremitte and Corbishley?"

"None that we have been able to establish," said Sloan, adding for safety's sake, "at this stage."

"If there's one profession worse than the Law for hedging its bets, Sloan, it's politics. Don't talk like either."

"No, sir." Sloan looked down at his notebook again. "I've also arranged for Constable Turton at Mellamby to start checking out whether anyone in the village there recognises the photograph of

Hamer Morenci. If he was really there on the day of the re-enactment as well as at the funeral, then it may be relevant."

Leeyes asked, "Did they sound the Last Post?"

"Not that I heard," responded Sloan repressively. The funeral service at Mellamby Church had been for Alan John Ottershaw, who had died in the Berebury and District General Hospital, and not for William de Wilton, Knight of the Shire, who had been slain on the battlefield of Lewes in 1264: but he did not say so. Thus reminded of something else, he said, "I have at last been able to make an appointment with the young doctor who treated Ottershaw in the Berebury Hospital. He's moved on to another area."

"Hoping he'll have something useful for you, are you, Sloan?" Like the late George Bernard Shaw, the Superintendent considered all professions a conspiracy against the laity.

Sloan took the question seriously. "Not really, sir. He thought Ottershaw had had a heart attack, treated him for one, and then certified that he'd died from one."

"Three bags full, eh?" Superintendent Leeyes scowled.

"And so did the Mellamby general practitioner, Dr. Lyulph."

"Game, set, and match," said Leeyes, "if you'd rather put it that way."

"I've also arranged to see the Dapifer——" Not liking his superior officer's expression, Sloan hurried on. "He was acting as a sort of steward the day Ottershaw died. Someone—but he can't remember who—was very anxious to know exactly whereabouts at the feast after the battle Bertram Rauly would be sitting. Kept on asking, he did. The Dapifer's trying hard to remember who it was."

Superintendent Leeyes sniffed.

"And," Detective Inspector Sloan produced a paper that had been lying on his desk when he got back to the Police Station, "we've had the report from the Scientific Laboratory on Ottershaw's clothing."

The Superintendent jerked his head up. "His costume, you mean."

"The material," said Sloan steadily, "had numerous superficial slashes visible to the naked eye."

"The sword-fight."

"But the fibres of the garment show clear evidence of having been penetrated with some force by something small in the region of the left chest."

"Makes a change, doesn't it, Sloan," said the Superintendent gratuitously, "getting something useful out of the scientists?"

A telephone on the Superintendent's desk rang before Sloan could reply to this. The senior policeman snatched at it and snapped down the line, "I thought I said I wasn't to be disturbed . . . What? What? What!" His normally ruddy complexion turned slowly to the choleric. "What's that?"

Someone on the other end of the line must have spoken in reply.

"What did you say?" The Superintendent's voice developed into a rising crescendo of disbelief.

The other person must have repeated the message.

That it was unwelcome was obvious even to a bystander like Sloan. An undefinable emotion suffused Superintendent Leeyes' face. Sloan thought it might be incredulity. Or anger.

"Say that again!" commanded Leeyes.

Something elusive in Shakespeare about news being thrice unwelcome hovered about at the back of Sloan's mind. But not for long.

The Superintendent slammed the telephone back into its cradle. "That was Turton."

"From Mellamby?" Sloan was already on his feet.

"There's been another fall of stone from the tower of the old Motte."

"And?" Sloan had his hand on the door-knob now. The Superintendent would never have been as excited as this just about medieval stonework. He knew that.

"And there's a body underneath it."

SEVENTEEN

And the Love of Dearest Friends Grows Small

IF DETECTIVE CONSTABLE CROSBY could have been said to have made good speed the last time he had driven from Mellamby to Berebury, it would have been grammatically correct to say that he made excellent speed back there. But the statement would not have done justice to the manner in which he accomplished the return journey to the village.

The Constable gave a virtuoso performance at the wheel, elevating the taking of a left-hand turning without losing speed to something approaching an art form. Any professional driver seeing Crosby's car going into a right-hand bend without either cutting the corner or losing momentum would have unhesitatingly awarded him an alpha plus.

Detective Inspector Sloan paid the Constable the supreme compliment of not giving his driving any attention at all.

True, he was hunched forward in the passenger seat and his eyes were apparently staring at the road ahead: but this was a case of appearances being deceptive. Detective Inspector Sloan's mind was fixed elsewhere.

On the fact, principally, that Constable Turton's message to the Berebury Police Station hadn't included a name.

To his alarm it soon became apparent that Detective Constable Crosby's mind wasn't entirely on the road either.

"Just as well I'd got back to the station, sir, wasn't it, before Colin Turton rang in," he said, sailing the car effortlessly past a juggernaut lorry. "Wouldn't have wanted you to have had to have another driver. Not when you needed a fast run."

Sloan hastily expressed his appreciation of the fact that Crosby had been available and immediately resumed his private contemplation of Constable Turton's message. Not only had it not included a name but it hadn't mentioned a gender either.

"There was plenty of everything at that funny farm place, sir," said Crosby, sending the police car skimming over a hump-back bridge at a speed that did its suspension no good.

"What funny farm?" asked Sloan absently, his mind still dwelling on what they might find at Mellamby Motte.

"Toad Hall, sir. That reptile aquarium over at Almstone. You name it and, if it's got scales, then they've got it. Starting with snakes and dangerous fish."

Sloan had almost forgotten Crosby's foray in search of sources of venomous substances that could bring about heart failure in human beings. With a real effort he wrenched his mind away from what might await them at Mellamby and back to sting-rays and suchlike creatures.

"With the research institute over at Pletchford, sir, it's frogs," said Crosby, starting to overtake a parked delivery van while not giving an oncoming double-decker bus the benefit of doubt. "They're into them in a big way."

Detective Inspector Sloan shut his eyes and for one blessed moment took his mind off murder, Mellamby, and marine animals and thought instead about his wife and son. If Crosby went on at this rate he might never see either of them again . . .

"But the Biology Laboratory at the University beats both of them hollow," said Crosby succinctly. "It's got everything including the poisonous hawksbill turtle."

"Scorpions?" said Sloan in what he hoped were his usual level tones. When he had opened his eyes again the bus was nowhere to be seen.

"Them, too," said Crosby, deftly skirting a group of bicyclists. "And mice. Thousands and thousands of them. For their experiments, they said."

Just at this moment Sloan found it difficult to consider an ordered world in which calm experiment was possible.

"Nearly there, sir," said Crosby equably. A model of co-ordination, he was a man in his element now, handling the supercharged police car with all the tenderness and intimate understanding of a lover. Man and machine became one as he slid the vehicle round the last bend into the village: to the marriage of such true minds Sloan was all in favour of the non-admission of impediments and he kept silent for the rest of the journey.

That there had been a fatality at the foot of the Mellamby Motte was obvious to Detective Inspector Sloan even from a distance. A quick *tour d'horizon* with his eye told him so. There was that about the grouping of the figures in the scene that could only betoken a death.

There were well-established laws of bystander activity in the case of assault—the more people there were about the less likely it was that any of them would come to the aid of the victim. There was, as usual, a converse to this law, too. A law of bystander inactivity which could almost always be invoked when someone had died and which bore no relation at all to the number of spectators. It related to an unnatural stillness—a sort of involuntary inanition—which always seemed to set in.

In fact the scene which greeted the two policemen as they approached the foot of the ruined tower could have been a *tableau vivant* but for one thing. A foot. There was nothing *vivant* about the foot.

It was sticking out from under some stones at a wholly unnatural angle, and Sloan, for one, was in no doubt at all that it belonged to a dead man. Nor was Dr. Brian Lyulph.

As if responding to an unseen theatrical direction the figures in the *tableau vivant* all moved a little when the two police newcomers reached the foot of the tower.

The doctor spoke. "There is no tibial or dorsal pedal pulse palpable, Inspector," he said. "I don't think even a Doppler monitor would elicit one either, and I have told Constable Turton so."

Sloan jerked his head, unsurprised.

"And from what we can make out there's no doubt that he's dead."

It wasn't, Sloan was sure, so much the Royal "we" that Dr. Lyulph was using; it was more a token acknowledgement of the presence at the scene of two veterinary surgeons and a one-time soldier.

Old Andrew Rebble pointed to the fallen masonry. "One of those lumps of stone would have been enough to kill a man, let alone the load that's come down on him."

Detective Inspector Sloan's gaze travelled from the dead man's foot to what he could see of the rest of him. He was quite sure that Sherlock Holmes could have deduced all he needed to know from a solitary shoe, but he, Sloan, didn't have time for that. All he could tell was that the shoe was laced and had once been highly polished.

Adrian Dungey said, "I started to try to lift some of the stuff off him but I stopped when I saw his fingers. They were dead white." The younger vet's hands were indeed scratched and dusty.

Police Constable Turton put in a comment that might have been a criticism too. "Very dangerous, that was, sir, until we know the tower is safe. For all you knew there might have been more wall to come down."

"The first rule of first aid," quoted Detective Constable Crosby with apparent consequence, "is to remove the patient from danger or danger from the patient."

As if with one accord every man there looked upwards at the ancient tower.

"I daresay he never knew what hit him," said Bertram Rauly gruffly. "A man wouldn't have stood a chance under all that."

"Not if he didn't see it coming," qualified Rebble.

"He wouldn't have done—not with this rough ground," said Dungey. "His head would have been down."

Sloan looked round the little group, conducting a mental roll-call. "Do we know who . . ."

Bertram Rauly, looking years older, said, "I'm afraid there's no doubt about that, Inspector."

"Didn't you know?" chimed in Dungey harshly. "It's poor Derrick Puiver."

SUPERINTENDENT LEEYES sounded almost incandescent with rage at the news.

Even though Detective Inspector Sloan was only talking to him over the telephone, he was as aware of the Superintendent's anger as if he had been standing in front of him at the Police Station at Berebury instead of sitting on a hard chair beside an ancient instrument in the entrance hall of Mellamby Place.

"Major Puiver!" Leeyes exploded. "Wasn't he the fellow in charge of that tomfool charade they had out there the day of the death?"

"He was the Battle Commander," said Sloan unhappily. He had elected to come up to the house rather than to use the police radio. Making responses through the medium of radio could be difficult. Exchanges of information in that way involved a distinct pause while the other speaker made use of the airwaves. Superintendent Leeyes was temperamentally unsuited to this. "As it happens," Sloan coughed, "Major Puiver chaired the political meeting the day before as well."

"What's that got to do with it?" demanded Leeyes. He sounded to Sloan as if he was actually bouncing about in his office. "Tell me that, Sloan."

"Nothing or everything," said Sloan tersely, adding with perfect truth, "I don't know which."

The Superintendent switched tack and enquired with more than a touch of sarcasm, "Anything masquerading as natural causes this time?"

"No, sir." Sloan was thankful that he could at least answer that firmly. The only possible way in which natural causes—at least Galileo Galilei would have called them that—could have been said at this stage to have come into Major Puiver's death would have been through the force of gravity.

"Or accident?" barked Leeyes, still sounding as if he would have to be scraped off the ceiling.

"We've been up inside the tower, sir, and made a preliminary examination of the masonry there."

"Don't hedge, Sloan."

"No, sir." He took a deep breath and carried on. "It isn't going to be possible to say, sir, without a detailed forensic survey whether or not the stone that came down was prised off and then pushed or just fell."

"Tell me the old, old story," rasped Leeyes.

Sloan hesitated before continuing. "I understand, sir, that the part of the parapet that has come down is called the chemise."

"I don't believe it."

"No, sir." Sloan wasn't sure that he did either, but Bertram Rauly had been adamant on the point. "There's a lot of loose mortar and stones still about up there on the top of the tower."

Leeyes still sounded peppery. "And did the victim just happen to be standing there below it?"

"I don't think so, sir. Major Puiver had told his housekeeper—he's a widower, by the way—that he had an appointment at Mellamby Place today."

Leeyes grunted. "But not that he was meeting someone dangerous under a fragile chemise."

"She says not."

"An accident going somewhere to happen?" suggested Leeyes ambiguously.

"Possibly, sir." Perhaps the Superintendent was working his way through the NASH classification of the four causes of death—horses for causes, Sloan's Police College tutor had called them, although Sloan hadn't ever known why. A braver spirit had ventured to ask the lecturer what he had meant and had been told that it was something to do with the Four Horses of the Apocalypse, but the class hadn't been any the wiser. There were certainly four causes of death —Natural causes, Accident, Suicide, and Homicide—and it seemed in this case that suicide was as remote as the first two.

That only left murder . . .

Leeyes growled down the telephone: it was at times like this that Sloan could understand how the instrument had come to be known in Cockney rhyming slang as the "dog and bone." "Wasn't that the same spot, Sloan, where the Member of Parliament had a narrow escape on their fun day?"

"It was." That very fact was not the least of Detective Sloan's concerns at this moment. It wasn't only the hard wooden hall chairs of Mellamby Place that were causing Sloan discomfort—flea chairs, Rauly had called them, on which the infested hoi-polloi of an earlier age could await their interview with the Lord of the Manor without leaving vermin in the upholstery.

"I don't like to be too obvious, Sloan," harrumphed Leeyes.

"No, sir."

"But I take it you have already asked yourself if the stone that came down could have been meant for the deceased on that occasion."

"I have," said Sloan simply.

"And?"

"And I don't know yet," responded Sloan steadily.

"You have also asked yourself, Sloan, I hope, if the first fall of stone could have been intended for the late Alan Ottershaw and not the Member of Parliament?"

"I have, sir, and it wasn't. At the time of that—er—incident Alan Ottershaw, in the part of William de Wilton, was having a memorable sword-fight with Adrian Dungey as King Henry III." That was an instance of using the word "memorable" in the narrow sense of being remembered.

Leeyes grunted.

"I will, of course," hurried on Sloan, "try to establish whether Major Puiver was anywhere within range of the tower at the time."

"Do that," commanded Leeyes.

"But," said Sloan carefully, "it might just have given someone else the idea."

"Talking of other ideas, Sloan, there's been a message for you from Ted Sheard. It's about the Select Committee on queremitte. He thought you might be interested."

"I am," said Sloan tightly.

"Its report is to be published tomorrow." Leeyes grunted. "I wonder what Hamer Morenci will have to say about it."

"We may have difficulty in finding out," said Sloan. "I got on to the Anglo-Lassertan Mineral Company straightaway—it was the first thing I did—and they say he isn't there."

"What? Then where is he, might I ask?"

"According to their people," said Sloan, "he left London last night for a business trip to Lasserta."

EIGHTEEN

But the Glory of the Lord
Is All in All

THE GIRL at the Anglo-Lassertan Mineral Company's head office was speaking nothing but the truth.

Hamer Morenci was indeed in Lasserta. He was ensconced in a suite in the best hotel in Gatt-el-Abbas. A young man from the firm's Public Relations Department who had accompanied him was already suffering. And not only from the heat.

The Chairman of the Anglo-Lassertan Mineral Company had first had a brief conference with a Malcolm Forfar hastily summoned from the minehead at Wadeem. Then he had been driven round to the Ambassador's residence.

Without preamble he said to Anthony Heber Hibbs, "So the Sheikh, having succeeded in getting us by the short and curlies, wants to make the most of it?"

"So I should imagine," said the Ambassador pleasantly, making a mental note to talk to the Chairman's aide about the importance of normal—if not excessive—courtesies in the Middle East. "And," he continued, "I should say that was—er—customary in the circumstances, wouldn't you?" Heber Hibbs waited with interest to see if Morenci was going to protest that international business wasn't like that; but the Chairman didn't say anything about things not being quite cricket and so the Ambassador carried on: "The good old public school tradition of waiting until a fellow's down before you kick him has always prevailed here in Lasserta."

Hamer Morenci looked suspiciously at Mr. Heber Hibbs. Employees of the great Anglo-Lassertan Mineral Company didn't speak with him as lightly as this.

"Saves a lot of trouble, doesn't it?" ventured the PR man nervously, "if you wait until the opposition's wrong-footed."

Morenci, whose alma mater was never mentioned in the reference books, transferred his baleful gaze to his employee, who quailed and retreated into silence.

"I understand from my Commercial Attaché," said the Ambassador fluently, "that Sheikh Ben Mirza Ibrahim Hajal Kisra is seeking further concessions from the company."

"He's imposing sanctions," snapped Morenci, "that's what he's doing."

The Ambassador opened the palms of his hands in the Thespian gesture of concession. It often came as a surprise to travellers that the law of supply and demand transcended national boundaries.

"We've got a cast-iron agreement," said Morenci.

"Let me see now," Heber Hibbs studied the ceiling thoughtfully, "wasn't there some little trouble about a breach of that agreement on the part of the Anglo-Lassertan Mineral Company a couple of years ago?"

"A mere technicality," blustered Morenci.

The Ambassador transferred his gaze to the carpet: service in the East being what it was, it was a very good Bahktiar carpet. "The Sheikh doesn't appear to be thinking on quite those lines."

"Ottershaw's dead," said Morenci. "Isn't that good enough for Ben Kisra?"

Heber Hibbs shook his head.

"He's had blood," snarled Morenci. "What more does he want? Human sacrifice?"

"It's not that," said Heber Hibbs. "It's the Select Committee."

Hamer Morenci said something which struck at the very roots of Parliamentary democracy.

"Very possibly," said the Ambassador mildly, "but I understand that the Lassertans have already had a whisper about the findings of the Select Committee in London."

"Have they, indeed?" said the Chairman of Anglo-Lassertan vigorously. "Friends at Court, eh? I haven't seen any report yet."

"It would appear," remarked the Ambassador, steepling his fingers

—putting statements into the passive case rather than the active one was a tool of democracy too—"that the Lassertans share the views of Her Majesty's Opposition about the high price of queremitte."

Sheikh Ben Kisra had, in fact, been considerably entertained when he had had the role of the Opposition in the House of Commons explained to him. The opposition to the throne of Lasserta—the survivors, that is—languished in the remote desert.

"High cost," responded Morenci automatically. "Not high price."

The PR man stirred. "The company's public image here, Mr. Ambassador . . ."

Heber Hibbs pulled down the corners of his mouth in a wry grimace.

"Not good?" said the PR man.

The Ambassador shook his head.

"Because of the accident?" queried the PR man busily. If he had a stock-in-trade it would be whitewash.

"The accident didn't help, of course," said the Ambassador fairly, "but even before that happened the company couldn't have been described as exactly popular in the Sheikhdom." He added, "Large foreign companies seldom are."

"Ah . . ." began the PR man eagerly. Such problems were meat and drink to men of his calling.

"What I want," declared Morenci, with emphasis on the personal pronoun, "is action. Not a lot of talk."

"I think," said Mr. Heber Hibbs suavely, "that in the first instance, anyway, you will find the latter more productive."

"You mean this banquet we've been bidden to?" said Morenci grumpily.

"At the Palace at Bakhalla tonight," trilled the PR man. "It's a dream of an address."

Morenci hitched a shoulder. "I suppose it's important."

"Very," said the diplomat, mentally beginning to draft a *note verbale* for despatching back to Whitehall. He thought he would begin by paraphrasing a famous dictum from the Foreign and Commonwealth Office. It had once felt obliged to comment that it was not the function of British diplomacy simply to be polite to foreigners.

"Hospitality has a ritual significance in the East," said the PR man. This much he did know.

"Indeed," said the Ambassador warmly. It had in the West, too, but Anthony Heber Hibbs did not say so. He toyed briefly with the idea of making a reference to Banquo but decided it would be lost on Morenci. "You may," he went on cautiously, "be invited to consume the unfamiliar and unappetising."

"I've had sheeps' eyes," said Morenci.

The PR man's face paled.

"And lived," said Morenci.

Years of training kept the Ambassador from making a direct rejoinder to this. Instead he said, "There is one dish, gentlemen, reserved by the Lassertans for special ceremonial occasions. It is only served as a mark of great rapprochement but, if it appears, there is some important advice which it is my duty to stress to the utmost."

"What's that then?" Morenci wasn't accustomed to either receiving or acting on friendly advice.

"If this particular dish is served it is absolutely vital that you chew every last morsel of it several times."

"Like Mr. Gladstone?" put in the PR man helpfully.

"If it's dangerous then I'm not eating it," said Morenci.

"It isn't dangerous but it would be impolitic as well as impolite to refuse their *pièce de résistance* however unattractive in appearance," said Heber Hibbs seriously. A State banquet obviously wasn't going to be the best place for West meeting East.

Hamer Morenci, the quintessential company man, braced his shoulders. "I can take it then."

"It is not so much a matter of taking it as of chewing it very, very thoroughly," repeated Heber Hibbs patiently. "I'll give you a sign if it comes up."

"All right, all right. Now, about what Ben Kisra is up to . . ."

"The Sheikh has heard—don't ask me how—that the Parliamentary Select Committee has been talking about the—er—undesirability of what might be called—er—circular relationships between civilian contractors and employees of the Ministry of Defence Procurement."

"We're clean," said Morenci flatly. "Company policy."

"In that case," said the Ambassador, "Sheikh Ben Kisra may argue that, if you're not paying out any bribes, then you're making too big a profit out of the Lassertans."

Morenci's face started to turn a nasty red colour.

"But what," intervened the PR man fussily, before his employer could speak, "does Ben Kisra really like talking about?"

"Birds of prey," said Her Majesty's Ambassador to the Sheikhdom of Lasserta.

"AH, SLOAN, there you are." Dr. Dabbe had reached the scene of Major Puiver's death by the time the Detective Inspector had got back from Mellamby Place to the foot of the tower. He shook his head. "A bad business."

"Yes, Doctor."

Dr. Dabbe waved his hand. "You might say that it's a case of one for his nob and two for his heels, mightn't you?"

"Pardon, Doctor?"

"I can tell you're not a cribbage player, Sloan."

"No, Doctor."

"Well, as you can see perfectly clearly for yourself, a large quantity of old stone has fallen from a considerable height on to the deceased." The pathologist grimaced. "And, until it is removed, neither I nor anyone else can tell you a great deal more about either the cause of death or its timing."

"We're waiting for the photographic people, Doctor," said Sloan in oblique explanation, "and more help."

"They're on their way," Dr. Dabbe assured him, adding innocently, "I overtook Dyson and Williams early on. And a heavy rescue unit and an ambulance a couple of miles back. No point in hanging about, is there?"

"No, Doctor." Sloan supposed he should be grateful that the pathologist hadn't overtaken Crosby as well: that wouldn't have done anything for road safety.

The doctor took a few steps back and said, "I'm afraid I can't even tell you if he was dead before all that secondhand masonry came down. Not until I've had a good look at him."

"Mr. Rauly said that he couldn't have known what hit him," proffered Sloan.

"That's what old soldiers always say," said Dabbe. "Good for morale."

"Yes, Doctor." As far as Sloan was concerned he supposed he might as well be bandying words with the pathologist at the scene of the crime as doing anything else. It was too soon for him to be able to read any of the alibis he'd sent for from everyone he could think of: even Hazel Ottershaw and Miss Finch. With something like a tyre lever even a woman could have prised off enough stone from the tower's parapet to start a real fall. At least, down at the Police Station nobody had ever taken the view that murder was men's work.

"He's as dead as a doornail, Sloan, anyway." The pathologist, too, had examined the protruding foot. "And quite coldish. Who found him?"

"The younger vet, Adrian Dungey. He was on his way to Mellamby Place to visit one of Bertram Rauly's dogs and noticed that there was something different about the outline of the parapet of the tower."

"What goes up must come down," murmured the pathologist absently, still regarding the foot. "It's where and when that matters, I suppose."

"No, Doctor," said Sloan firmly. He was wholly serious now. "It's the 'why.' "

"Let's hope you do find a motive, Sloan," responded the pathologist with equal gravity. "Murder without motive is the most dangerous power game of the lot." He waved a hand in the direction of the Motte. "One of the ruins that Cromwell knocked about a bit?"

"Slighted by the Parliamentarians was how Mr. Rauly put it, Doctor."

"Right but repulsive," said Dabbe.

"Beg pardon, Doctor?"

"The Roundheads, Sloan. They were right but repulsive."

"Were they, Doctor?"

"And the other side were wrong but romantic—the Royalists."

Sloan stiffened. "Say that again, Doctor."

Dabbe stared at him. "Say what again?"

"That bit about the other side being Royalists," said Sloan softly.

"Dammit man, you heard me the first time. The Civil War was between the Parliamentarians and the King's Party. The Royalists."

"That's what I thought you said, Doctor. And the Battle of Lewes was between the Baron's side—that is Simon de Montfort and his pals—and the King's party."

"You know it was, Sloan. That's all old hat. Besides, you told me so yourself. It was what the re-enactment was all about. What's worrying you?"

"I missed something," said Sloan. He looked down at the Major's protruding foot, suddenly chilled. "Something that was right under my nose." He raised his voice. "Crosby, come over here a moment. I want you."

DETECTIVE INSPECTOR SLOAN had never been in this sort of a Chase before: at least not in the variety of woodland that had once upon a time provided good hunting for a king.

King John, he thought Bertram Rauly had said. He'd been a bad king, hadn't he? The bold barons had made him sign on the dotted line—or its medieval equivalent—in a field called Runnymede and then, as every schoolboy knew, King John had gone and lost his baggage train with the Royal treasure in it in the Wash.

A simple pun on the name of an East Anglian delta had stuck far longer in Sloan's mind than any scholarly lecture delivered in the classroom. There must be a moral there somewhere.

He was sorry his quarry had taken to the woods. He must have heard Crosby being called and then seen the two policemen walking purposefully towards him.

And put two and two together and taken to his heels.

He'd left the others still standing in an uneasy group and shot suddenly northwards, skimming the water that downstream became the River Pletch and plunging into the Mellamby Chase.

Sloan and Crosby had started to run after him, but he'd gained ground early on and by the time the two policemen reached the wood the man was nowhere to be seen. Behind him Sloan was dimly aware of the rest of the group bringing up the rear—but slowly—rather as the body of the hunt follows the Master and the Huntsman.

They were chasing a man who had the cunning of a fox and the fleetness of a hare and it wasn't easy. Almost at once it became considerably more difficult. The forest way divided.

"You go left, Crosby. I'll take the right fork." He shouldn't have been panting quite as soon as this, surely?

Crosby loped off obediently and was lost to sight almost at once although Sloan continued to hear him lunging through the trees. What he should have done, of course, was to send Crosby back to report and to summon up reinforcements, although it would take a small army to search the Chase. Derrick Puiver's mind would have worked that way. Sloan thought about the poor little Major who was dead now and who shouldn't have been, not if he, Christopher Dennis Sloan, had had his wits about him. He couldn't think how he had come to overlook something so glaringly obvious. Perhaps it was because everyone had told him about it.

Trees not planted by the hand of man had a random quality about their distribution which hindered pursuit. Sloan ran on, checking himself at the point where he saw a broken twig. He had chosen the same route through the forest, then, as the man whom he sought: which was a comfort. But had the man chosen to leave the track and lie low, then he, Sloan, might even be running away from him.

That applied, too, if he had climbed a tree like King Charles II. An oak tree that had been, hadn't it? And in consequence numberless children had celebrated Oak Apple Day ever since.

Sloan noticed another snapped twig, this time on the ground.

So he was still behind him whom he sought—he hadn't overshot the mark. Sloan travelled onward as quickly as he could, as alert now as any huntsman of old. He was without a weapon though and that might be important. He would just have to do what the Assistant Chief Constable called playing a cadenza and improvise.

From somewhere behind him in the Chase he could hear someone calling him: the words had a familiar ring but it was a full half minute before he caught their import.

"Yoicks! . . . Yoicks! . . . Tallyho! . . ."

Unless Sloan was mistaken that was a spiritual descendant of the de Caquevilles giving voice to an ancient hunting cry that too came directly from the Norman French incitement to hunt of *Trout tro ro rot illocques illoloco.* So must the Chase have resounded in olden times at earlier hunts when the aim was sport and food.

What Sloan was pursuing was justice.

"View halloa!" bellowed Bertram Rauly from somewhere to

Sloan's left. That meant he'd heard something, didn't it? Rauly must have made good speed for an older man, but then he knew every inch of the Chase.

Sloan could hear Crosby's voice, too, faint but pursuing. "He's coming your way, sir."

"View halloa!" repeated Bertram Rauly lustily. "Tantivy!"

Sloan veered in the direction of the hunting call. Didn't it mean "found" in hunting parlance?

Then Sloan saw where their quarry had left the main path—his tracks still showed in the forest carpet. He'd doubled back, which was how he'd been seen by the others. Sloan followed almost without thought. In fact, oddly enough, it was the Assistant Chief Constable's definition of a cadenza that occupied his mind: a passage for a solo instrument at or near the end of a movement, sometimes improvised.

Sloan froze.

He'd rounded an ancient oak and there in the middle of a little glade stood his man, preternaturally still, only his eyes moving.

For a full moment neither hunter nor hunted moved.

Then Sloan saw the man's right hand move quickly to a pocket. Summoning up all his strength, the policeman flung himself forward in a flying tackle just as Detective Constable Crosby came plunging out of the undergrowth, Bertram Rauly hard behind him.

"Adrian Dungey," Detective Inspector Sloan addressed a figure on the ground, "I arrest you for the murder of Alan John Ottershaw."

"And Derrick Puiver," said Detective Constable Crosby.

NINETEEN

Dominus Illuminatio Mea

"I'M WAITING, SLOAN," said Superintendent Leeyes.

"Yes, sir."

"I take it you do have an explanation?"

"In a manner of speaking, sir." He hesitated. "I'm not quite sure exactly where to start."

"In the beginning," thundered Leeyes. "Like Genesis."

"Yes, sir." He toyed for one wild moment with the idea of saying "Adam and Eve and Pinch-Me" but put the thought out of his mind almost immediately and said instead, "It all began with a simple road traffic accident in Gatt-el-Abbas in the Sheikhdom of Lasserta."

"Simple?" growled Leeyes, who, like the Foreign Office, always favoured the conspiracy theory as a first option. "Are you sure?"

"As sure as we can be. Accidents do happen."

"Not according to the psychologists, they don't," maintained Leeyes stoutly, "but go on."

"The Sheikh of Lasserta immediately saw some mileage in the accident from his point of view—a chance of putting the screws on the company and so forth."

"The ability to see where the advantage lies is the essence of successful business," pronounced Leeyes.

"Very probably, sir." That sounded to Sloan suspiciously like a quotation from an Adult Education Class on "Business and the Community." "When the Sheikh started making threatening noises the company withdrew Ottershaw as quickly and as quietly as they could."

"We know that," said Leeyes impatiently.

"We knew it later, sir. The trouble was that they didn't tell anyone at the time."

"Why should they have done?" asked Leeyes.

"It might have helped, sir, if he'd telephoned home before turning up there."

Leeyes grunted. "Like that, was it?"

"I'm very much afraid so," he said. "And I should have spotted it earlier."

Leeyes said nothing.

"When I interviewed Mrs. Ottershaw," said Sloan, "she told me that the first thing she knew of her husband's being back in the United Kingdom was when she heard his key in the latch."

"And that was true?"

"As far as it went," said Sloan. "It would have been better if someone had got up to bolt the door." Perhaps the old ballad had had more meaning than he'd realised.

"Flagranti delectissimo," pronounced Leeyes with all the vigour of a man who had some Latin and no Greek. A little bit of bread and no cheese was what Sloan's mother had called that.

"Precisely, sir. Poor Ottershaw now had two things to worry about. My guess is that he put the domestic difficulties on ice during the day on the Saturday and got on with seeing about the Lassertan end of things. After all that was literally a matter of life and death or, if not that, at any rate his job."

Leeyes grunted. "And he wasn't to know that the Mellamby end of things was going to be a matter of life and death too."

"No." Sloan frowned. "I don't think that ever occurred to him. By the end of the Saturday afternoon he'd seen Peter Corbishley and felt that he'd got somebody really rooting for him."

"Marvellous, isn't it," said Leeyes, "how these politicians always manage to give that impression? And what had been going on with the two Members, might I ask?"

"Oh, that was something quite different." Sloan turned back the pages of his notebook. "I'm afraid, sir, that comes under the heading of experimental psychology."

"So does sparing the rod and spoiling the child."

"This purported to be a study of the effects of autosuggestion on two local public figures by an undergraduate called Richard Godstone for his dissertation. Unauthorised, of course," added Sloan hastily. "His tutor was apologetic but not unbearably surprised."

"Death and his brother, Fear."

"Er—quite so, sir." St. Francis of Assisi wouldn't have liked that: nor would Sloan's mother. "Anyway, it didn't work. Neither Member was deflected from his duty."

"Or scared to death?"

"No, sir. I gather the students were very disappointed that Ted Sheard didn't even mention the harassment when he addressed the Social Psychology group at Almstone College. Peter Corbishley didn't propose to, either."

"I suppose they didn't think windbags could be tough," said Leeyes uncharitably. "They'll learn. But it was nothing to do with the Ottershaw affair?"

"My theory—it's only a theory, mind you, sir, because Hazel Ottershaw isn't saying anything to anyone—is that Alan Ottershaw devoted the Saturday evening to seeing what could be done on the domestic side. The trouble is that Adrian Dungey did the same thing with a very different end in view."

"Murder?"

"Very clever murder."

"Well, he is a professional man."

Sloan let this calumny on education pass. "He went out to Toad Hall—he is their vet, anyway—and collected some venom from the kokoi frogs there. Colombian Indians use it as an arrow poison."

"So he's spilled the beans," concluded Leeyes.

"Yes, sir." The attractive boyishness of Dungey was a thing of the past now but he was willing—anxious, even—to tell the police how clever he had been. "This venom has an effect on the heart similar to that produced by a heart attack and is known as batrachotoxin."

"And is what went into the pellet?" said Leeyes.

"Yes, sir. It was then lightly sealed in with a wax that has a low melting-point."

"Thought of everything, hadn't he?" sniffed Leeyes.

"Nearly," said Sloan. "If the queremitte was found, someone from the Anglo-Lassertan Mineral Company was bound to be suspected first."

"Supplied by Hazel Ottershaw?"

"She's not saying."

"And if the ashes were interred as planned nobody would have been any the wiser."

"Yes, sir. The beauty of the scheme was that the pellet would have been delivered back to the undertaker."

"So it was curtains for Ottershaw all right."

"Yes, sir." The swishing together of the curtains was what Sloan didn't like about cremation. "After seeing the Member I think he must have gone into the question of reconciliation with his wife."

"It never works," commented Leeyes, not one of nature's optimists.

"It didn't—at least as Hazel Ottershaw declines to comment, we can only conclude that by early on the Sunday morning Alan Ottershaw—rightly or wrongly—had decided that the situation would be best resolved by his going back to Lasserta."

"Next best thing to being a *mari complaisant* if you ask me," said Leeyes trenchantly.

"I don't think so," said Sloan. "You see, sir, he'd got something else to do first."

"What was that?"

"Beat the living daylights out of Dungey."

"Good idea," said Leeyes warmly, "but——"

"That's what put me on to him in the end," said Sloan, "but I should have got there sooner." He supposed that was the lament of all detectives.

"Are you going to tell me, Sloan, or shall we go on playing guessing games?"

"Adrian Dungey was playing King Henry III at the re-enactment and Ottershaw stood in as William de Wilton."

"Well?"

"At the real Battle of Lewes, sir, they were both on the same side. King Henry and William de Wilton should never have been fighting each other like that, should they?"

• • • •

"DIDN'T GIVE THE SWORD-FIGHT a second thought myself," admitted Bertram Rauly, "although it did cross my mind that I couldn't have given the King the pasting that William de Wilton did." He looked squarely at Sloan and Crosby. "It was a sort of play within the play, wasn't it?"

"Like *Hamlet,*" agreed Sloan.

The landowner stroked his chin. "And the falling stone from the tower?"

"The first time," said Sloan, "the students who were harassing the Members of Parliament pushed one block over just to shake Peter Corbishley. He was in no real danger. In fact, when we came to look closely at all the incidents relating to the Members of Parliament, one of the things that stood out was that nothing really happened to either of them. As my constable pointed out, if injury had been intended they'd have been sent letter bombs, not anonymous letters."

Crosby squinted modestly down his nose.

"The second stone fall, of course," said Sloan, "was quite a different matter."

"But why kill poor Puiver? He didn't have anything to do with Ottershaw or Dungey," said Rauly.

"No, sir," said Sloan, "but Major Puiver had said publicly that he had recognised Death's walk—which indeed he had. I fear Dungey took advantage of that. What the Major couldn't remember was where he had seen that walk before—but, of course, it had been the previous day when the same man had been heckling Peter Corbishley."

"So that's what it was." Rauly's brow cleared. "And it would have been him who did that funny bit of bone-pointing under the platform party."

"Most probably, sir."

"But why kill poor Puiver? He had nothing to do with Ottershaw."

"To put us off the scent."

"A diversion?" Former tank commanders understood about diversions.

"I think so, sir. It must have been obvious that the police were on to something or we wouldn't have been round asking questions. He probably thought he ought to widen the field for us."

Bertram Rauly stroked his chin thoughtfully. "Dungey was the Camulos Society's armourer, so the technicalities wouldn't have been difficult for him. He had the expertise."

"He had access to the poison, too," said Sloan.

"I didn't know there were so many frogs in Calleshire," said Crosby feelingly. "Or mice."

"The other matter which doubtless concerned him no end was how much Alan Ottershaw had committed to tape when he rang his firm."

"Worrying for him," agreed Bertram Rauly in a voice devoid of sympathy.

"I think Dungey just kept the queremitte pellet in his pocket until the right moment presented itself," said Sloan.

"And then," supplemented Crosby, "popped it into his crossbow instead of a plastic dye one."

"Nobody would have noticed in that mêlée," commented Rauly. He raised an eyebrow. "Very nearly the perfect murder, eh, Inspector? Oh, by the way . . ."

"Yes?"

"I think I've settled Miss Finch's hash."

"You have, sir?" Sloan looked up with real interest. "How?"

A wicked look came over Bertram Rauly's face. "I offered to leave Mellamby Place to her. Haven't had a squeak out of her since."

"NOT . . . ?" Mrs. Heber Hibbs' eyes widened in spite of the ever-present Middle Eastern sunshine.

"Yes!"

"But he didn't just swallow it, did he?" Like the admirable wife that she was, Mollie Heber Hibbs was listening with flattering attention to her husband's account of the Sheikh's banquet the night before for the Chairman of the Anglo-Lassertan Mineral Company. Women played no part in Lassertan hospitality.

"He did," said the Ambassador.

"Perhaps," shrugged Mollie Heber Hibbs kindly, "he thought he should because he was the guest of honour."

Anthony Mainwaring Heber Hibbs was not prepared to ascribe

any such sense of duty to Hamer Morenci. "All he did," he reported accurately, "was to pretend to chew it."

"That's no good, is it?" responded his wife loyally.

"None."

"But you had told him, darling, hadn't you?"

"Several times," said Mr. Heber Hibbs. "I told him that I would indicate if the dish were to be served. And I stressed the importance of chewing that particular course very, very thoroughly, giving signs that he was enjoying it. If he could."

Mollie Heber Hibbs stared at him, still wide-eyed. "Didn't he listen, then?"

"He listened," said her husband judicially, "but I don't think he heard."

"What about the nice young aide he had with him?"

"The PR man? Oh, he was all right."

"He chewed it, you mean?"

"No. When he heard what it was he fainted."

Mollie Heber Hibbs instantly became all concern.

"Someone had told him," said her husband, "that they were to be served a great delicacy."

"That shouldn't have——"

The Ambassador said solemnly, "The PR man asked what it was—in the line of duty, I suspect, as much as anything. Probably thought it would look good in the company's Annual Report or something."

"But that——"

"Someone translated it as the liver of freshly killed kid."

The laughter lines on Mollie Heber Hibbs' face crinkled. "And he thought——"

The Ambassador carried on with equal merriment. "He asked if the Lassertans were cannibals and they didn't understand the question. They thought he was asking them how the young goat had been killed. And when they told him," finished Heber Hibbs, "he fainted."

"Poor fellow."

"You'd better keep your sympathy for Hamer Morenci," said the Ambassador. "He's feeling very sorry for himself. And only after eating raw goat's liver, too."

"I'm not surprised. His throat all swollen and his ears so painful."

"He can't speak yet," said Heber Hibbs, adding judiciously, "Perhaps it's just as well. At first if he could have done he would have been spitting fire. At the moment," he added brutally, "all he's spitting is blood."

"And tongue-worms by the hundred." Mollie Heber Hibbs shivered. "It's funny how they thrive in the human mouth."

"The doctor says they're *Linguatula serrata* from the goat's liver all right, and that he'll be as right as rain in a few days. On the other hand Morenci says—or, rather," the Ambassador amended this in the interests of accuracy, "Morenci writes that he'll never be the same again. The chap even manages to write angrily. Interesting, that. He wanted to ask the Sheikh to give him his present back, too."

"Not that lovely Audubon painting?"

"The gyr-falcon," said the Ambassador dreamily. "The one I advised. Much as I should like the Anglo-Lassertan Mineral Company to have a watercolour of *Fallo gyrfalco* on their hands surplus to requirements, I told him that, if he did, that would be the end of the company's mining concession in Lasserta."

"I thought he was very subdued when I called at the hospital this evening."

"Chastened is the word," said Heber Hibbs. "He'd heard from London by then of course about the murders in Calleshire. Our precious Chairman is so glad to be off the hook over them that he's going back as soon as he can to act on the Select Committee's recommendations." The Ambassador stretched out easily in his own armchair. "Ah, well, everything is relative, I suppose." He cocked an enquiring eye at his wife. "Did I say that or was it Mahomet?"

"Confucious, probably," said Mollie Heber Hibbs comfortably. "It almost always is."

"Give me the China Station any day," said Her Britannic Majesty's Ambassador to the Sheikhdom of Lasserta. "By the way, I've asked that young PR man round to luncheon tomorrow."

"I expect he's at a bit of a loose end with his boss in hospital and speechless."

Heber Hibbs sat back and said lazily, "Not only that but I've had a great idea for an advertising slogan for his firm. I want to put it to him."

Mollie Heber Hibbs was not deceived. "Tell me . . ."

"Arms for the love of Allah."